Alone
in the
Wilderness

The story of a present day Native American high school student who is challenged to spend three months alone in the Beartooth Wilderness Area of Montana, living as his ancestors had lived.

Hap Gilliland

Library of Congress Cataloging-in-Publication Data

Gilliland, Hap
    Alone in the wilderness / by Hap Gilliland
    p. cm.
    Summary: A Native American high school student is challenged to spend three months alone in the Beartooth Wilderness Area of Montana, living as his ancestors had lived.
    ISBN 0-87961-257-6
    1. Cheyenne Indians—Juvenile fiction. [1. Cheyenne Indians—Fiction. 2. Indians of North America—Montana—Fiction. 3. Beartooth Mountains (Mont. and Wyo.)—Fiction. 4. Survival—Fiction.] 1. Title.

PZ7.G4153 A1 2001
[Fic]—dc21   2001042717

2005 printing

Naturegraph Publishers has been publishing books on natural history, Native Americans, and outdoor subjects since 1946. Please write for our free catalog.

Naturegraph Publishers, Inc.
3543 Indian Creek Road
Happy Camp, CA 96039
(530) 493-5353

Books for a better world

Dedication

To Shantel Sellers (Cherokee), Rita McFadyean (Blackfeet), Tobie Wright (Comanche-Potawatami), Sally Old Coyote (Crow), and Jon Reyhner (Indian Education Specialist) in appreciation for their careful scrutiny and excellent suggestions.

To Hugh Huntley, John Moore, Jeff Barton, and all of the other good friends who have taught me much during more than twenty-five backpack trips into the Beartooth Mountains Wilderness Area.

And most of all, to Erma, who cheerfully puts up with my wandering spirit, my need for adventure, and long hours at my laptop computer.

Contents

1. The Challenge..5

2. The Decision..11

3. The Old Way..29

4. The Preparation..43

5. The Sweat Lodge Ceremony..59

6. Alone..65

7. The Hunt..75

8. The Climb...85

9. The Quest...99

10. The Grizzly...115

11. The Blizzard...127

12. Missing...137

13. The Rescue...145

1
The Challenge

Three whole months alone in the wilderness? Facing blizzards, and grizzly bears, and who knows what? Three months without seeing another person! What made me think I could do that? I've never even been in the wilderness! I must have been crazy to agree to it.

Of course, I've done lots of hiking, climbing rocks, and watching animals near my home on the Cheyenne reservation. And I've always dreamed of someday exploring the high mountain country, living the life of my ancestors, but those were dreams of the distant future. That is until this morning.

What made me say I could do it? Maybe it was my frustration with trying to adapt to a city high school, and the attitudes of many of the students. Transferring to a new high school in the middle of the semester can be devastating, especially if you have a name like Flint Red Coyote and you are moving from an Indian reservation to a city school. I was struggling in most of my subjects. The only saving grace was my advanced biology class. We were studying mammals and the instructor really knew his stuff. He knew the science. I knew them from experience watching them, and following their tracks.

Tobie Wright sat at the other end of my table in biology. I considered her a good friend. Although we had never once talked to each other, she always smiled at me when we passed in the halls. Sometimes she'd give me the high sign or wave at me from a distance. But she was as enthused about biology as I was, so we communicated during discussions. A wink, a shake of the head, a thumbs up.

Tobie was enthusiastic about everything, even American History! I hated history. Mr. Johnson, the teacher, seemed to agree with the history book. I don't think he thought of Native Americans as people. We were, as the textbooks taught, only obstacles to progress, to the settling of America. Roger, Frank, Thomas, and their friends didn't help the situation. A crew of local boys, they were always telling jokes or making snide remarks about the Indians, and they usually glanced in my direction when they did it. I learned to just ignore them, tune them out, along with the teacher. That was how I coped, until this morning, when they were discussing the "first Thanksgiving."

I was sitting in class, not paying much attention to what was being said, wishing I was back on the Cheyenne reservation with my friends. I only had one friend in Billings besides Tobie. Jose Gonzales and I had been in fifth grade together in Butte. He had just moved up from Mexico and we had become best friends, so I was glad to discover he was now in Billings. But we didn't have much chance to get together outside of class, because he worked at McDonald's after school.

I don't think I had said two words in any class during the three weeks I had been in Billings Senior High, until this Monday morning when I heard Roger ask the teacher, "What in the world did they think they were doing, anyway, inviting Indians to their Thanksgiving feast? The Indians were their born enemies. It was bound to lead to trouble!"

I was getting fed up with that kind of remarks, so I blurted out, "If it hadn't been for the Indians, the Pilgrims would have all been dead!"

"Why? The Indians were their only enemies!"

"Except starvation! The Indians gave them corn and squash and tomatoes. Taught them how to grow them. Taught them everything they needed to know. The Pilgrims were from England. They didn't know a thing about surviving on their own in the wilderness. The Indians were the experts on living in the wilderness. Still are!"

"Still are?" Thomas almost shouted. "Present-day Indians couldn't survive in the wilderness any better than I could. I'll bet you couldn't find a person on your reservation that could survive if he got lost in the wilderness."

"A lot of us could," I said. "We still have the know-how. It's handed down from our grandfathers."

"You?" Roger sneered. "You ever been in the Beartooth Wilderness? I'll bet you ten bucks you couldn't survive in those mountains for a week without freeze-dried food and modern equipment. Especially this time of year!"

I usually stop and think carefully before I speak. It's the Cheyenne way. That's why I never speak up in class. Teachers don't know you should think before you answer. But although ten dollars might not be much to Roger, it was a fortune to me. And I was getting hot under the collar. "Sure, I'll bet with you. I could go up there tomorrow, take my bow and arrows, and live off the land, just as my ancestors did!"

"Boy, now there's a bet! Let me see your money. Here's my ten bucks!" Roger pulled a ten dollar bill out of his pocket and slapped it down on his desk.

"Mine too," Frank said, pulling a billfold from his pocket.

"Here's mine," others chimed in.

I glanced at Mr. Johnson, silently pleading with him to call a halt, to declare that this had gotten out of hand, that it wasn't part of history class. But he didn't. He just sat there with a grin on his face.

Jose stood up at his desk on the other side of the room. "How many want in on this?" he asked. That really surprised me. Jose was my friend! Maybe he thought he was supporting me!

I glanced around the room. Most of the boys were half out of their seats, as if they were ready to pounce on me. Three of them were waving money over their heads. I doubted any of them were serious. They were obviously trying to force me to be the one to back down.

The girls were staying out of it, sort of laughing to themselves, or whispering to each other. All except Tobie. Tobie winked at me and gave me a little nod of encouragement, as though she were saying "Don't back down. I'm rooting for you."

"How many?" Jose said again. "Put 'em up high!"

Nine hands waved in the air.

"You know I couldn't cover all those bets," I said.

"You don't have to," Jose said with a grin. "Personally, I'm sure you can do it, but I'm betting that you can't. That makes ten of us, and we'll all bet our money against your ten. That makes it ten to one. Okay fellas?"

A couple of them hesitated to give me the ten to one odds, but I guess they felt like they couldn't back down if the rest were willing. When they all nodded their heads, Jose added, "Just to prove we're serious, we'll all give our money to Mr. Johnson, to hold till you get back."

Mr. Johnson hesitated too, but finally nodded his head and said, "If you really mean to go ahead with this, I guess I can hold the stakes."

Then Roger spoke up, "I've got a car. I'll take you up there and drop you off—pick you up in a week."

"Just a minute," I said. "I don't mind betting with you, because I know I can win—but there's no way I'm going to miss a week of school. I had trouble enough transferring from the Lame Deer school in the middle of the year. I'm not going to flunk out of school just to prove something to you guys."

Mr. Johnson broke in. "Now you're talking good sense. Why not do it the week after school's out. I'd like to see how you come out."

"Now you're talkin'," I said, thinking how much fun it would be to spend a few days in the high mountains.

Frank spoke up again, "A week in the summer? That won't prove a thing about bein' able to live off the land. Anybody can fast for a week. It don't take none of the old skills to do that."

This could have been my way out, but I was still thinking what a great excuse it would be for spending a week, or even the whole summer in the high country. Maybe I let the euphoria get the best of me. It would be a chance to follow out my childhood dreams. Once again, without taking time to think seriously about what it entailed I proposed, confidently, "How about three months?"

Everyone looked surprised, and skeptical. Even Tobie tipped her head to one side and raised one eyebrow. I also thought, however, that some of the boys looked at me with a little more respect, and after they had all looked at each other, they nodded their heads. It appeared that everyone was agreeable until Roger spoke up. That's still summer. I know some guys that could do it in the summer, at least for a while. But you said you could do it this time of year—winter."

"How about September to December?" Frank ventured. "That'll give you all kinds of weather, both summer and winter, to prove what you can do."

"Yeah, try that on for size," Roger said with a sneer. "I suppose you think you could do that!"

I thought I heard a couple of laughs. I was sure they all thought I would back down this time. Then they could really sneer at me.

Jose shook his head, as if he meant to say "Don't agree to it."

But Tobie raised her eyebrows, and her lips said, "Do it."

This time I took a minute to consider. It was a tough assignment, but I was feeling pretty self-confident. With all those eyes on me, expecting me to admit it was too tough for me, my ego wouldn't let me back down, not right now anyway. I said okay, we had a deal.

"Wait a minute," Mr. Johnson said. "What about your priorities? That's school time too. You just told us you wouldn't miss any school on this wild goose chase! I'm not holding any bets that will keep you from graduating."

Here was another out, and I knew I should take it. But when I glanced at Tobie and saw her nod of encouragement, and felt Jose's anticipation from across the room, I said, "After this school year, I'll only need one more semester to graduate. I can do that spring semester, and still finish in June."

Roger walked to Mr. Johnson's desk and slapped down a ten dollar bill. "Okay fellas. Now put up or shut up."

As some others started forward, Mr. Johnson said. "Just a minute now. If I'm going to hold the stakes I want to know the terms. Flint you said you'd take a bow and arrows. What else?"

I tried to think fast. "A tent and a sleeping bag. There aren't any buffalo robes now. A little food to get me started, until I can do some hunting."

"Let him take anything he wants, as long as he takes it in by himself," Roger proposed. "He can't carry too much."

The others nodded, and Mr. Johnson said, "All right, give me your stakes. I'll put the money in the bank till next fall, so no one can back out."

"I'll have to give you mine in a week or so," I told him. "I just got a part time job at the stockyards Saturday mornings. I don't know yet when I'll get paid."

2

The Decision

It's one thing to accept a challenge when you're defending yourself, and the culture of your people against the doubts and ridicule of your classmates. It's quite another thing to face up to what you have said you can do when you are thinking about being alone for three whole months and facing the worst that nature has to offer. What would it be like in those mountains in the winter? Blizzards? Forty-below weather? And me in just a tent?

I love hiking and climbing, and I've always been confident of my abilities along those lines. But I couldn't help wondering if the bravado I showed in class was misplaced. I should have just stuck with one week, or just the summer.

Nothing was said about my potential trip before history class the next day. As usual, all the guys just ignored me. Maybe they had pretty much forgotten about the challenge, but I sure hadn't. I sat there in class, thinking more about it than Mr. Johnson's lecture.

When I looked across the room at Tobie, I could see big flakes of snow drifting down past the window behind her. I wondered if next year would be as nice and mild as this year, or would it be one of those years when the temperature dropped to zero long before Thanksgiving. How much colder would it be up in those Beartooth Mountains?

My family lived in a little old house in a rundown section of town about two miles east of Billings Senior High School. With five of us living in our little three-room house, and with my sister's six-year-old son, Jake, running all over, there really wasn't a decent place to study at home. I took the bus to school every morning, but instead of catching it back home, I usually went to the school library to do my homework, then I walked home. If Jose wasn't working, we would both study then walk home together. But today I decided that I would ride the bus to keep out of the storm. I would try to do my school work at home.

I kept glancing over at Tobie, wondering if she was being friendly because, like me, she was one of the three whom the white kids called "different." Jose was obviously Mexican, and anyone could tell I was an American Indian. But what was Tobie? I hadn't the slightest idea. Her kinky hair that hung uncontrolled to her shoulders, would have made her look African, except that it was light brown, and her face had none of the African features. Her slim face had the high cheekbones of a Native American. Were her strong, tanned arms and legs a sign of race or of a healthy lifestyle? Her well-proportioned figure could belong to a girl of any race. I had plenty of time to study her face in class because she never looked in my direction. She was too busy concentrating on the teacher and every word he was saying. She didn't notice that I was paying more attention to studying her and to the snow coming down outside the window behind her, than I was to Mr. Johnson's lecture. Tobie didn't even glance in my direction as she left the classroom.

As soon as the last class was over, I stuffed a couple of books in my day-pack and hurried out to the bus stop to be sure and get a seat before the bus filled up. The storm had ended, but there was snow on everything. It was cold, and I wasn't about to let someone else get my space on the bus.

I stepped back from the curb to avoid getting sprayed with slush by the passing cars. Someone touched my arm and a pleasant voice said, "You can't ride a bus on such a wonderful day as this." I turned and looked down at Tobie's smile. "Come on Flint. Let's walk home through the park."

"What park?"

"Pioneer Park. It's right north of the school. Haven't you been there?" Tobie didn't wait for an answer. She whirled around and repeated "Come on." She started off, and I hurried to catch up.

We walked around the school building, past the football field, and into the park. Tobie stopped and exclaimed, "Isn't it gorgeous!" About three inches of fresh snow covered the lawn. Every limb of the spruce trees held a load of snow, and it was even piled up on the branches of the huge cottonwood trees. It truly was splendid, and was made twice as beautiful by Tobie's enjoyment of it. She took my hand as we walked through the snow. Then she released it as she rushed forward to study some small animal tracks.

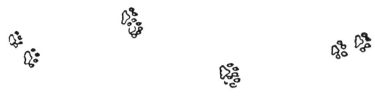

"Just cat tracks." She was disappointed, but she followed the tracks anyway. "Must have seen a bird," she said, as the tracks suddenly were far apart, showing that the cat had leapt forward in great bounds. "Or maybe this dog frightened it," she said, pointing to another set of animal tracks.

"I don't think so," I answered. "That dog's no bigger than the cat. How did you know it was a dog's tracks, not another cat?"

"By the claws," she said playfully. Then she turned and grinned at me. "Just testing me, aren't you!"

"And you passed with flying colors!" I said with a laugh.

We followed the dog's tracks a short distance till they crossed a man's tracks. "I wonder if that man was looking for the dog," I said. "If he did, he didn't find the dog's tracks, cause he got here before the dog."

"Maybe he was just taking a shortcut across the park"

"I don't think so. The man was searching for something", I pointed out. "He didn't slow down, but see how he looked behind every bush he passed, every place an animal might hide?"

"No, I don't see. How do you know where he was looking?"

"Look at the angle of his foot when he puts it down. See how he turns his right toe out when he looks that way?"

"How did you learn to understand tracks like that?" she asked.

"Grandpa expected me to see everything. Not just see what the animal was doing, but to think of the way it was thinking. This wasn't too hard in the winter, when there was a light snow like this, but it was tough in the summer."

"You tracked in the summer?"

"Tried to. When I'd think there were no tracks, Grandpa would tell me to look farther ahead and see the difference in the way the light reflected from the grass that leaned in the direction an animal was moving. He spent hours teaching me to watch for those little details. Several times he had me out all day, coming back to the same set of tracks that were made at dawn, so I could see how the tracks changed, and know how old they were. We did it both summer and winter. I wish I understood tracks as well as he did."

Tobie leaned down to study a track. "These can't be squirrel tracks. The front feet would be side by side, like those of other tree climbers. Yet they're pretty small for a rabbit."

"A small cottontail," I said. "Probably a young one from a late summer litter. Cottontail usually have two litters if food is plentiful."

We walked on. "What's this?" she asked, pointing to some tracks.

"I don't believe it," I said as I followed the tracks across the park until they crossed a little stream. "It really is. It's a raccoon." I pointed out the big hind-foot track, and a part of a front foot, like a little hand. "I'm surprised to see a raccoon in the middle of the city."

"I'm not."

"You're not?"

"No. Yesterday I heard two girls talking about someone's pet raccoon that had wandered off."

"Maybe you can show them the tracks and help them find it. Maybe if it ran away from them it was in the wrong home to begin with. Maybe it's better off in the wild. Be sure you learn about the people before you send it back!"

"I envy your knowledge of the woods, and your understanding of animals." she said. "But mostly I envy the experience you'll have in the Beartooths this fall. I hope it really works out well. I know it will. I wish I could go with you!"

I didn't answer right away. The idea made my heart pound. Oh, how I wished I could take her along. I had never known anyone else who stirred up the feelings of kinship that she did. Finally I said, "I told them I could do it alone."

"And that's what you'll do. I was just wishing. It wouldn't work if I went. People wouldn't understand. Probably not even my parents. The dominant culture is all tied up with sex. They don't understand a real friendship between a man and a woman. Anyway, I don't think I have the skills to do it. You do."

We walked on through the park. I liked the look of admiration she had given me, but I knew very well that a real friendship wasn't built on false pretenses. "I sort of went overboard when I told the class I had all the skills I needed. I was defending the Native People in general. I really don't know that much. Grandpa Red Coyote, my dad's father, was teaching me all the old skills, as a grandfather is supposed to do, but he died when I was in the fifth grade. I haven't learned much since. The last time I hunted with a bow and arrow was the day of his funeral. I went out and shot a wild turkey for the feast that followed it. I don't know if I could hit the side of a barn any more. I don't even have a good bow."

Tobie looked up at me and smiled. "I looked at next semester's schedule yesterday. There's an archery class. I hear the instructor is really good. Sign up for it."

"And admit to all these guys who are watching me that I'm not already a skilled archer?"

"Don't look at it that way. Tell anyone who mentions it that you're supporting the school's instruction of a Native American skill. And if it's important to you, you'll become the best. Don't worry about it." We stopped to look at some more tracks and she said, "I was sure you could help me with the tracks. Apaches are great trackers, and Granddad was one of the best, but my family lived in the city. When we did get out to visit Granddad on the reservation, he tried to teach me everything he could about tracking. But there was never much time. I'm still trying to learn as much as I can."

"So you're Apache! I wondered."

"A quarter. Dad was half Apache, half African."

"Then that's where you got your kinky hair! From your Black ancestors."

"Not Black, African! Dad tried to teach me about both cultures. I value all the parts of my heritage. I don't want to lose any of them. But it's been much harder to get accurate information on the African part."

"I hope you can learn some Zulu dances. I think they're the most spectacular dances in the world."

"Oh, then you understand! Maybe someday you can teach me some Cheyenne steps. I love pow-wows. They're a wonderful way of maintaining some of our traditions, as well as being a lot of fun. But the dances here are a little different from the Southwest's. Do you have a pow-wow on the Cheyenne reservation this summer?"

"Yes. Fourth of July. Maybe you can come?"

"You can bet on it."

"Oh, no! No more bets for me," I said, and we both laughed.

We came to the edge of the park and she said, "Want to walk a little farther?"

"I'd love to," I said as I took her hand in mine, and we walked on.

Most of the walkways had already been cleared, but a block or so up the street one was still covered with snow. An old man who must have been in his eighties was shoveling the walk from his house toward the street. He was moving slowly. It looked like he could hardly push the shovel, let alone lift it filled with snow. I hesitated. If I had been alone I might have offered to help him. Tobie walked straight on, not looking to either side.

Just as we passed by he put down his shovel and turned toward his house.

Tobie gripped my hand tighter and stopped me. As soon as the man was inside his house she said, "Come on." and headed up his walk. "There's a broom by his door. I'll get that, you take the shovel. It won't take us long."

After we had his walkway cleared, we started on the driveway. Tobie kept glancing my way with a grin on her face. "Want to trade tools for a while?"

"No. I'm doing fine."

As soon as we finished the driveway, Tobie took our tools and set them beside the door. She had a grin on her face and a sparkle in her eye as she said, "Come on. Let's get out of here before he catches us."

I put my arm around her shoulders and she slipped an arm around my waist, and we strolled on without saying a word. She finally broke the silence by saying, "Too many people think you can't communicate with your friends without talking. They have to be chattering all the time."

"Yes. And they think good friendships have to be between men, or women with women. I'm really glad you and I can be friends."

"Me too," she said. "But it's got to stop right here. Now!"

"What! Why?"

She glanced at my face and laughed at me. "Don't look so shocked! I just mean for today. I've got to get up to the University. They have a better research library than the high school, and I have a report due tomorrow!"

With that she spun from under my arm and headed north without another word, or even looking back.

It was Thursday afternoon, two days after my stroll with Tobie. I rode the bus home from school because my sister, Dolly, had the day off and she wanted me to get home early so I could take care of Jake, her six year old son, while she and Mom went Christmas shopping.

While Jake was taking a nap, I sat down with a sheet of paper and started listing all the things I would need if I really did go to the Beartooths. I knew sleeping bags were very expensive. So were tents that could be heated with a backpack stove. And how much fuel would I need? I could never carry enough or build a fire inside a tent, and I'd need heat. I could build a fire in a tipi, if I had one, which I didn't. Well, my lack of equipment could be an excuse to get out of the whole deal. I could just tell them I didn't have the ten bucks for the bet, or the money to get the equipment I would need, which was the truth.

Talking about three months in the wilderness had been great. The whole idea was exciting. But to actually do something about it scared me, even just writing a list. It made me face up to what it would really be like, and how unprepared I was. And, therefore, how crazy!

I hadn't been working on my list five minutes when the door opened and my dog, O'kohome, shot through. Grandfather Wolf Runner was right behind.

"Grandfather!" I shouted, "when did you. . ." I started toward them, but I was bowled over by my dog's affectionate charge. I gave O'kohome a big hug. I had sure hated to leave him on the reservation with Grandfather, but we didn't know if we'd get a house where they'd allow dogs.

I struggled back to my feet and took Grandfather's hand in a firm grip. "How did you get here?"

"Walked."

"All the way from the reservation? A hundred miles?"

"Henry Knows-His-Horses was going to Hardin. He gave me a ride that far. That's only forty-six miles from here."

"Isn't there a bus?"

"I'd rather walk. You know I like to walk. Anyway, the bus won't carry a dog. Then he looked at me. "Someone told me you were going to spend three months in the Beartooths. You'll need O'kohome."

"Yes, I'll need his company, and his help pulling a sled, if I can find one I can use. I can't carry everything I'll need for three months. But how did you hear about it already? It's only been three days since I first talked about it."

"The reservation grapevine works pretty fast."

"Well, I'm not going till September. That's if I go at all. I've been wanting to talk to you about it. Here, give me that blanket, and your jacket. Have a chair so we can talk."

"If you want to talk serious, sit here," he said, motioning to a spot in front of him as he lowered himself to sit cross-legged in the middle of the floor.

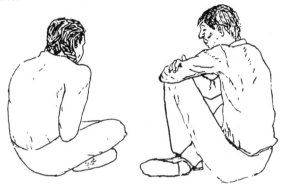

Before Mom and Dolly got back, I told Grandfather about how I had gotten into this whole mess. I said, "I told the class I had all the old Cheyenne skills I would need, but when I had time to think about it, I realized I really don't have the skills."

"What do your parents say about it?"

"Dad says I'll probably learn a lot. But I don't like the way he says it! Like I don't know anything! Mom is pretty hesitant. She says she can't advise me. She says I'm supposed to go to the tribal elders for that. That's why I was wishing I could get down to the reservation and talk to you."

"Your Mom's right, but the elders can't make the decision for you. Never could. We can give you lots of good advice that you should consider carefully, then make your own decision. Remember that. Elders can advise you because they have lots of experience. But the world is changing so fast that we sometimes wonder if the old knowledge is any good now. Just be sure you pay attention to the people who have real wisdom. There are a lot of people giving bad advice these days. Especially to young people. Maybe you've been listening to too much of it."

Suddenly I was sorry I had asked Grandfather. I was positive he was going to tell me I was being foolish, and I shouldn't go. That made me realize for the first time how very much I really did want to go. I wanted the adventure. It was the biggest thing in my life right now. But I had asked for grandfather's advice, and I would have to listen. I thought a minute before I said, "Maybe you're right, but I'd hate to back out now. I'd really get razzed by all the guys that are betting I can't do it."

"Are these good friends? Real friends? The kind that would go all out to help you be prepared? If they're not, don't pay any attention to them. Don't let them influence your decision at all."

"No, they're not really friends. More like enem . . . . no, I guess they're what you always call *potential* friends."

"What about your real friends?" Grandfather asked.

"I've only been here a short time. You don't make friends quickly in the city, but you remember Jose. He was my best friend in Butte, in the fifth grade. He talks real encouraging. He wants me to do it, but he keeps telling me to be sure it's safe. He doesn't want me to take any big chances. Then there's Tobie! I think Tobie'd be heart broken if I backed out now."

"Tobie, huh?" Grandfather raised one eyebrow. "Who's this Tobie?" Someone serious?"

I didn't know how to answer. She was more mystery than anything else. "She's a friend. A good friend. She may have too much confidence in me. She makes me feel I could do anything."

"And you can," Grandfather said. "That is if *you* believe in it, too. But only if you *really* believe it. . .Why do you want to do this, anyway? Just to save your pride?"

"No," I said. "I guess it's the adventure. I don't know. Maybe it's the challenge."

"Challenge! Now you're talking Cheyenne. The opportunity to prove yourself."

I nodded.

"In the old days, every young man took on a difficult task to prove himself. Today, too many young men don't ever take the challenge. They look at the world the Native American lives in, and give up. They're afraid to go after it with all their heart. In my day, they would have been called cowards. We'd have dressed them in women's clothes and let them skin the buffalo and scrape the hides. Those who were going to be real men didn't hesitate. They took the challenge. They ignored their fear and it went away."

"What kind of challenge?" I asked.

"Anything that took courage, that would build their self-confidence for whatever they had to face in life. Sometimes in the old days a young man would count coup by riding into a battle and touching an enemy warrior with his coup stick. Or several boys would go to an enemy camp and steal a bunch of horses. Stealing horses was not robbery. It was the football game between the tribes, proving that your team was better than theirs."

Grandfather sat up straighter than I had seen him in a long time. His countenance took on the vigor of a young man. I knew he was picturing himself in the old days, in the presence of warriors. He went on, "By the time I was your age, the horse stealing days were over. So I went out to capture a wild stallion. I made up my mind almost a year ahead. I practiced every day, till I could run all day."

He stopped and looked squarely at me. "What are you doing to get yourself in shape?"

"I run the two miles home from school most nights. But sometimes I take the bus, like tonight."

"Do you think that's enough to get you in shape for carrying a pack up a mountain? If you want to do anything right, you've got to be prepared. . .As I was saying, I went after this wild stallion. A good man can outrun a horse. A horse can run faster, but a man has more endurance. A modern-day horse that lives in a pasture wouldn't be too hard to catch, but this stallion was the leader of a band of wild horses. I ate pemmican as I ran. I drank from the same water holes he did. When I laid down to sleep a couple of hours, he rested, too. It took me ten sleeps to catch him, but I finally got my rope on him. I stayed there and broke him to ride. Rode him several times a day till he learned to trust me. I didn't go back to camp till I had him gentle. We became inseparable. He saved my life twice through his loyalty."

Suddenly I was excited about the whole idea. I had a new outlook. If I accepted the challenge I was part of the old Cheyenne culture. Maybe I could do everything the old way, equipment and all. And maybe Grandfather could help! "If I do it, will you help me get ready?" I asked.

"Well, I'll try to teach any of the old Cheyenne ways that might be helpful. It is good that you are not going on your challenge soon. You have to be ready mentally, physically, and spiritually. All three are essential to the success of both your challenge and the vision quest that should precede it. I can at least help you prepare for your vision quest. No young man went out on the challenges I was talking about, till he'd been on our vision quest, and knew his spirit helper."

Now I really got skeptical. He and I were talking about two different things. "I'm not talking about a vision quest," I retorted. "I know that was important long ago, but no one does that anymore. Nobody believes in it!"

"I know. Even by the time I was growing up half the guys didn't do it. The white man said it was just superstition. Because they were told that, some of those who went didn't have visions, but those of us who went gained a great deal. It influenced our whole lives."

"Well, that's not what I'm talking about. I want you to teach me some of the skills I need to survive, and help me make the materials."

"I can teach you the old culture, the values, the spiritual things by which you should live. These things last a lifetime, and they'll serve you wherever you live. But I've forgotten most of the old skills, that I haven't used. Your Grandpa Red Coyote lived with your family. He taught you a lot of skills like tracking animals, and hunting with a bow and arrow, didn't he?"

"Yes, but he died when I was in the fifth grade. Remember? I haven't shot a bow since. I'll need to be really good to get my meat this fall."

Grandfather reflected on my words. "That's only five years ago. I haven't shot a bow for over fifty years. I don't think I can help you."

I hesitated to tell him this, but finally I said, "I could sign up for an archery class at the high school spring semester. But it's taught by a white man."

"Good. Good. Don't ever hesitate to learn from anybody. No group or culture has a monopoly on knowledge. To get along in this world, we have to learn all we can from everybody. Maybe two cultures are better than one. If you have two, you can choose what fits you. Just don't forget your Cheyenne values, and make sure you make the right choices."

I shook my head and said, "You sound just like Tobie!"

That evening, after Grandfather had gone to bed, I told Mother a little about my conversation with him. I said, "I learned a lot, mostly about the importance of taking the challenge and putting my heart into it, but he also caused me to have more doubts. I had thought he could help me learn some of the old skills, like my other grandpa used to do.

But he claims he doesn't think he can remember them. All he wants to teach me about is the culture and the values. Will you talk to him?"

Mother turned and glared at me so I had to look down. After a minute she said, "Young men are not supposed to talk like that about their elders. You're supposed to speak with respect. Maybe the Cheyenne values are what you really need to be taught!"

After lunch the next day, Jose and I sat in the cafeteria and talked. I told him that I would be a fool to go ahead and plan for that wilderness trip, but I just couldn't get it off my mind. I wanted to do this more than anything I had ever done. I had always wanted to live the life of a trapper or a woodsman, something that would give me a chance to live like my ancestors for awhile. But I needed more experience before I tried it. I had never even had an opportunity to go backpacking. Why should I pretend that I knew all about it, or was an expert?

When he saw my doubts he said, "I'm sorry I got you into it if you don't think you're ready to do it, but I figured you'd be jumping at the chance. I was sure you had all the skills. You sounded so confident in class. I also remembered how you showed me up at climbing those rocks around Butte back in the fifth grade."

"Sure, I've done a lot of rock climbing and tracking around home. But the only time I ever really camped was in a cave in a canyon once. We went there on horseback, and not with backpacks. I've slept in tipis at pow-wows, but that's not really camping, " I told him.

"Maybe you haven't had as much experience as I thought, but you know a lot about it. Remember that time I spent the day on the rez with you? You showed me how to climb up through that rock 'chimney' to get to the top of the ridge above Lame Deer. And you shot the wild turkey."

"That's not like camping in the mountains and living off the land for three months," I said.

Jose still thought it was a great idea, and was willing to help me prepare any way he could. I might have given up the whole idea if it wasn't for him. Well, him and Tobie.

As we went to our next class I asked Jose, "Have you noticed that Tobie isn't in any of the morning classes? I never see her around school before lunch."

"I heard some of the girls talking about her earlier this fall. It seems that she is in some kind of a program for highly gifted students, doing mostly independent studies. They said she had chosen to take the American history class because she wanted to know more about the European-American heritage."

"I'm glad she likes biology too," I said, "or I suppose she wouldn't be in my biology class."

The statement kind of slipped out. I hadn't realized how it sounded. I glanced over at Jose's face. He just raised one eyebrow and grinned at me.

I thought about Tobie a lot more than I should have. I don't know why she was on my mind so much. I had never really talked to her except that afternoon when we looked at the tracks in the snow. It wasn't that she was especially pretty. A lot of the girls were more beautiful in a surface kind of way. But I was intrigued by her kind eyes, her alert expression, her attentiveness to everything that went on, and her quick laughter when she and the other girls talked together. The smile and greeting she gave me as we came into class boosted my ego, no end. I'll admit that Friday afternoon I sat there looking over at her and day-dreaming more than listening to Mr. Johnson.

Then, as we left class Tobie stopped me. "How do you get your exercise?" she asked. "Do you like to run?"

"I run home from school most nights," I said. "That's two miles. But Grandpa says that's not enough."

"Ever run stairs?"

"Stairs? Well, uh, no."

"I like the stairs. Keeps me in shape for mountain climbing."

"I guess it would," I agreed. "It's probably what I need."

"I have Friday nights after school free, so I run the stairs. Want to meet me right here after school?"

For once I didn't stop to think before I answered, "You bet I do." Once she was gone, I wondered what I was getting myself into.

She was waiting for me at the classroom door when I got there. "Where are your books?" she asked.

"Books? Uh. What books?"

"Don't you have homework?"

"Yes, but they're in my locker. I thought we were running first."

"You know they don't allow running in the halls, or the stairs, at the high school. I go up to the university. Come on, we'll go by your locker on the way out."

We walked the mile to the university campus in silence most of the way, just enjoying each other's company. I followed Tobie into the university library. She set her day-pack with her books in it on a table, saying, "They'll be safe here till we finish running."

We walked over to the Liberal Arts building and took the elevator to the top. "I start up here," she said, "so I can warm up going down. I run down three flights, then up two. Down three and up two. By the time I get to the bottom, I'm warmed up and ready to really exercise. So, I run up three and down two. By the time I go down and back up three times that's three hundred flights. Come on!"

I wasn't quite in condition for it, but I managed to stay with her. I think I slowed her down a little at the end, but she didn't mention it. As we walked back to the library she said, "By spring we'll want to do it with our day-packs on. Maybe add a few extra books. Now let's look at that history assignment. By the time we do it you'll be rested up for that long run home. The assignment's for the week but we can make a good start on it." She seemed to already know all about the subject, and when we finished discussing it an hour later she had saved me several hours of reading.

Before I finished putting my books in my day-pack and had my jacket on, Tobie had more books stacked in front of her and was concentrating on one of them, but she stopped studying long enough to say, "See you in class, and back here next Friday!" I took off on a run, but I only ran till I knew I was out of sight!

The next day was Saturday, the day the Billings stockyards had their cattle sales. I felt very lucky to have gotten a part-time job helping move the calves and the steers into the sales ring where the auctioneer auctioned them off. I liked working with the animals. This Saturday they gave me my pay before I went home. I told the history class that I would bring in the ten-dollar bet when I got paid, but I hadn't been able to buy any Christmas presents for my parents yet. They had to come first. I rode the bus out to Rimrock Mall and did my Christmas shopping.

When I headed down the hall to my history class Monday morning I was trying to decide just how I would explain not having the money. I wasn't going to say that I might not go—not yet. If I did, Mr. Johnson might say that I was showing good sense, but not the boys in the class. They would all call me chicken, and I'd deserve it. They'd be razzing me about it the rest of the year!

I didn't know if I should be angry or relieved when, no one said even a word to me. Everyone just ignored me, as they always had. Except Tobie. She gave me a smile and a thumbs up as I walked by her desk.

All week I kept hoping that I could talk to Tobie after history class, but she was either gone out the door and down the hall before I had a chance, or some of the girls were grouped around her and I wouldn't interrupt. I figured if she wanted to talk with me she would make an effort.

Friday was the day to run the stairs, so I looked for her after school but I didn't find her. I thought about going home, but decided I would go by way of the university. I walked into the library and sat down at the table where Tobie and I had studied. I pulled a book out of my pack but I didn't open it. Then Tobie walked in and greeted me with a big smile. "I hoped you'd be here," she said.

"And I hoped you were coming, but you didn't say anything this morning."

"I didn't want you to feel pushed. I wanted it to be your choice."

After we had run our three hundred flights of stairs, we walked back to the library to study. Tobie said, "You said that your grandfather was the one who helped you learn the old Cheyenne skills. Since he's gone, do you have anyone who can help you make the things you'll need in the Beartooths?"

"I know I gave the impression that there were still plenty of Cheyenne with the old skills but there are not that many, and they're on the reservation. I thought my other grandfather, my Mom's dad, Grandfather Wolf Runner, could help me. But he's not much interested in the old skills. I think he thinks we don't need them any more. He's more interested in the values, the culture, the spiritual side of the Cheyenne life. I do know how to tan hides with deer brains, to make a tipi. But I'd like to make other things like my own bow and arrows. The bow that Grandpa Red Coyote helped me make when I was in fourth grade sure isn't good enough for me now. And I don't have the know-how. I'm sure there's someone else on the reservation who could help me, if I were there, and they had the time, but, well, I suppose I'll just have to buy what I can find, if I can save up enough money. But I'd rather have the old Native American kind."

Tobie looked at me for a minute. "There's plenty of help around, if you're just willing to admit you need it." She studied my face a minute before she went on. "I was going by the school shop before school this morning, so I stepped in and looked around. The teacher came over and I asked him if a student in the spring semester class could make things like a bow, or a sled, or snowshoes, and he said, 'Sure. If they have some basic woodworking skills they can pick their own projects. I'll help anyone who really wants to learn.' "

I looked at her and laughed. "Taking good care of me again, are you? While I sit and wonder and worry, you act!"

"I've watched you. You don't question teachers. You wouldn't have asked."

"You're right. and I appreciate it."

"I know it's difficult. You follow the old Indian ways a lot. And that's good. But remember, you have two cultures. Pick the best from both of them. When the white culture works the best, you've gotta use it. Speak up, like they do."

"You sound just like Grandpa Red Coyote. He taught me all the old skills, but he insisted I learn the new, too. He helped me practice flint napping till I could make really good flint arrowheads. But then he insisted I go down to the trading post and buy good steel ones to hunt with. Some of the skills he taught me can never be replaced."

"Like tracking," Tobie said.

"Right!"

3

The Old Way

"Yes," I said. "I do plan to go to the Beartooths. I really want to do it. But if I go, I want to do it the old way. So I'll need your help."

Grandfather looked at me for a long moment, then a grin came over his face as he asked. "The old way? What is the old way?"

That's a silly question, I thought, as I gave the obvious answer. "The way the Cheyenne people used to do things."

Grandfather sat, thinking, then finally began. "You say you want to do everything the old way, and that is good, because there are many good things that have been forgotten. But there is no definition of the old way. Our culture is changing. All cultures are changing. They were changing a thousand years ago. They would have changed even if the Europeans had never come here. Some of the changes are good. Some are bad. Are you talking about the way the Cheyenne people did things five hundred years ago when we lived north of the Great Lakes and had never heard of buffalo or horses? Or maybe the way your great grandfather lived before we got steel knives or matches? Or is it the way your grandparents lived, or your parents, or the way we did things three years ago?"

He paused to let me think a minute before he went on, "Yes, it is important that we learn the values and the ways of our ancestors, so we can preserve and honor the good things. But we can't bring back everything. No one knows everything our ancestors did. As the outsiders moved in, we accepted some things and lost others. Our grandfathers lost a lot. Our parents lost a lot more. For some of our children, only a small trace of the old ways is left. There are some new ways and new things you will want to accept and take with you, just as your great grandfathers accepted the horse and the rifle. Some of the old skills will be very important in the wilderness, like telling directions and time by the stars and predicting the weather by the formation of the clouds and the way the smoke rises from your fire. But some of the old ways must be folded up and put away, as we do with our old clothes. They can be taken out and worn for special occasions. But you can never do everything the old way, because you can't even define it.

"Yes," he continued, "I'll help you to learn as many of the old ways as I can. But there are many old skills that I never learned, or have forgotten. You know many of the old values. I'll teach you others. But you have to choose the ones that fit you, just as you will have to use some of the newer skills and materials. They have become part of our culture." Grandfather stopped and laughed before he said, "Your children will call these the old ways!'"

I hoped Grandfather would start right away teaching me some of the things I might need to know for my backpack trip, but instead he started telling me some of the old legends. I started to object, but then I remembered that I had told him I wanted to do things the old way. That was how he had been taught the values of our people when he was a child.

The Friday before Christmas Mr. Johnson told us our main test for the course would be Tuesday, the day before vacation started. We'd better be prepared. Tobie wasn't in either biology or history class that day. I'd never known her to miss class. Could she be sick? Probably she wouldn't be there for our exercise and our study time either! I looked for her after school but didn't find her. Feeling rejected, I loaded my history book and my notes into my pack and walked slowly toward the university campus, not even noticing if there were new tracks in the park as I crossed it. When I walked into the library, head down, someone said, "What are you looking so glum about?"

I looked up and exclaimed, "Tobie!"

"I didn't think you'd be here!" Both of us said it at once, then we both started laughing.

"But where were you at class time?" I asked. "I was worried about you."

"I was being interviewed for a special project."

"Oh? What kind of project?"

"You'll hear all about it, if I get it, but there's no use talking about it until I get the answer. There are thousands of top students applying for it, but I'm optimistic."

"You always are!" I said as I set my pack on the table and asked, "Do you know we are having our big semester test in history Tuesday?"

"I heard," she said. "But let's go run the stairs. The exercise will clear our brains. Then we can talk about the test."

When we got back to the library after our run, Tobie sat down across the table from me and asked, "Are you still worrying about that backpack trip?"

"I don't know if I should follow my heart and go. . .or use my brain and back out. Grandfather is visiting us, and I thought he'd help me decide, but he only confuses me."

"What does your grandfather say about the trip? Does he think you shouldn't try it?"

"No. He thinks it's a great idea. But he doesn't want to help me prepare. He won't really talk about the skills I need. He says it's my challenge. Like a young warrior going out to prove his bravery and earn his place as a warrior. Then he tells me stories about great Cheyenne warriors like Mouse's Road."

"Tell me about Mouse's Road."

"Well, he and three other young Cheyennes went out to prove themselves by stealing horses from an encampment of Kiowas and Comanches. They got the horses, but a big group of Comanche warriors came after them and caught up with them.

"The four Cheyennes rode to the top of a hill, killed their horses, and got behind them. But when they were attacked, they ran out of arrows and three of them were killed. Mouse's Road jumped up and ran after the attacking warriors. A Comanche chief, who rode a fine horse, charged him with his lance. Mouse's Road ducked under the lance, caught ahold of it, and wrenched it from his hands, throwing the chief from his horse. He killed the Comanche chief then took the lance and defended himself in the next attack. Then he ran after his attackers.

"Neither the Comanches nor the Kiowas had ever seen a man as fierce and swift as Mouse's Road. All their weapons seemed useless against him, so they turned and ran away. A few of the braver ones stayed and signaled in sign language to Mouse's Road, who had mounted the dead

Comanche's horse. 'Wait, we'll give you a saddle, and you can go back to your camp.'

"Grandfather told me about other young warriors going out on their challenges to prove their bravery. He talks of this wilderness trip as my challenge as a young warrior. He must think it will really be dangerous. And he's probably right. It might not be for an experienced woodsman, but I've never even been on a backpack trip."

Tobie grinned at me and said, "Those young warriors had never been on a raid either. I thought you were like me, that you liked to do things that were different, that you jumped at the chance to do things that you'd never done before, that no one else did."

"You're right," I said. "Ever since I was a little kid, I've liked to explore new places on the reservation, and do things I'd never done before. I always spent twice as much time as the other kids hiking around, climbing rocks, exploring the back areas of the reservation, tracking animals in winter. Most of the kids wanted to do things they were sure of. They wanted to follow the same paths they had always walked. I always figured if I have been on the trail before, if I know it, that's a good reason to take a different one. It makes life a lot more fun. It gets me in trouble, too, sometimes, especially in school like in math and science classes. The teacher shows us one way to get an answer. I want to understand their way, yes, but then I start experimenting to see if I can get the answer by another route."

"That's what great scientists do. Like Einstein."

"Yes, but teachers don't like it."

"I don't let that bother me. I want to spend my life trying new things, learning new cultures, going to places most people don't even know about."

"So do I. I'd like to go to Kyrgyzstan, in central Asia. I understand they have the same kind of picture writings on their cliffs that we have here in Montana. I'd like to visit the Massi in Africa and hear their folk stories. I hear they are very much like some of our Cheyenne legends."

"There are a lot of kids who have those dreams," she said. "But they don't have the git-up-and-go, the gumption, the determination—call it courage. They'll never do any of it. They want the adventure, the excitement, but they'll settle for getting this from books and the Adventure Channel. Nothing any more hazardous than Disneyland's Jungle Cruise, and video games. All manipulated pseudo thrills, substitutes for the real thing. That's how we are different from the rest.

How we're alike, you and I. We don't want to live in that artificial reality. We want the real thing. And we'll get it."

"Traveling the world doing the real thing costs a fortune," I reminded her. "I don't have any money. Probably never will!"

"I don't have any either. But you're talking about tourist travel. I wouldn't go on a tour even if I had the money. I want to go to a country, move in with the people, live with them, learn their culture, live it. And there are ways to earn your transportation. I'm already looking into it. But that's my future. You've got a chance to do something here and now!"

"If I have enough experience, enough knowledge to do it."

Tobie thought a minute and said, "Experience—or gumption? Your grandfather calls it bravery. I'd call it determination. People in every culture need it. It's a lot more important than training or experience. I was just reading about Admiral Byrd and his explorations in the Antarctic. Have you heard about how he survived a whole Antarctic winter alone in a little cabin hundreds of miles from any other human?"

"Yes, but he had the knowledge and experience."

"Not as much as some of his crew. Several of them had more arctic experience. Some had more training. And they were physically stronger. Byrd didn't even drive dog teams. He was more interested in finding the meaning of life. But the others wouldn't have made it. They didn't have the determination. Well, one of them did—Norman Vaughn. Byrd respected Vaughn so much that he named a mountain he discovered after him. Vaughn had always been determined to climb that mountain, but he never had a chance until almost seventy years later. In spite of a fused ankle that wouldn't bend, and a heart pacer, he just recently climbed that mountain. When he was ninety! Those two weren't any better prepared for what they did than the young warriors your grandfather told you about. What all of them had was determination. What about you? Are you determined? Or are you looking for an excuse to get out of it?"

"No way!" I said. "I want to do it worse than anything I've ever wanted. I just want to be sensible."

"All of our great explorers, scientists, and even our great Native American leaders, have done things that everyone else said was impossible. People said they were crazy to try. If you're worried about survival, it only takes four things: food, water, heat, and determination. Call it courage."

"Well, I think I have that," I told her.

"Grandfather says I should go on a vision quest first, but no one does that anymore."

"No one goes out and risks their lives living alone in the wilderness any more either. But you said you were determined to do this and do it the old way. Go for it!" She thought a minute and said, "You'll want to climb at least one of the high mountains, too. I climbed Dewey Peak in the Beartooths last summer. It was great. When you get to the top of a peak, think of me!"

Tobie dumped her books out on the library table. With them was a folder of papers. She picked it up and said, "Here, you might want this. I had it with me for that meeting this afternoon."

I looked at it. "Northern Arizona University? What's this?"

"An application. Have you decided what college you're going to go to?"

"College? I haven't even really thought about it. I won't graduate until the end of next year."

"Neither will I—if I get my special project. But we've got to plan ahead."

I wasn't ready to think about *more* school. "I don't know if I could get in."

"Don't count on just one. Apply to several places. I've already been accepted by the Center for Excellence in Education at the University of Arizona. We don't want to get left out, do we? You know we can do anything we want if we plan ahead and really work for it!"

"Like pass this test Tuesday?"

"Yes. Look, I know it's personal, but do you mind showing me your history notebook?"

"I don't take very good notes," I told her. "I was planning to study mostly from the book." I shoved the notebook over to her.

"There's too much in the book. And Mr. Johnson's tests are mostly from his lectures, or the parts of the book he's talked about. You've got to study the teacher as much as the book." She pushed my notebook back in front of me and said, "What you've got is fine—what there is of it! Just go over your notes carefully. I've got something else to do." She took two rolls of dimes out of her purse, picked up her notebook, and headed for the other end of the library. It wasn't long before she was back with a stack of papers. She laid them in front of me and said, "Those are copies of all my class notes. Study them carefully before Tuesday."

For the next two hours she sat across the table and did research for another class, but stopped to answer my questions whenever I had any. Finally she reached across the table and put her hand on mine. She looked at me for a minute then said, "Flint, I need your help. Something only you can do for me."

I was surprised. What could I possibly do for Tobie? I looked into her face. "Of course, Tobie. Anything. What can I do?"

Tobie pulled three little Apache Indian dolls from her pack. We looked them over. They were beautifully made with buckskin dresses and delicate beadwork. Tobie said, "They were given to me when I was in the third grade. We had just moved from the reservation. I had always had my good friends around, and now I had to face Christmas alone in the city, where I knew no one. You know what it's like. I was devastated. But three people remembered, and sent these dolls to me. They made such a difference! Made me feel loved. I have treasured them ever since." Tobie handed me a card with three addresses on it. "These three little girls are new in Billings. Their fathers are out of work. There will be no Christmas for them. They all live down near North Park, your neighborhood. I want you to take the dolls to them."

"Are the girls Apache?"

"One's Crow, one Blackfeet. I don't know about the other." She grinned at me. "Maybe Cheyenne." She helped me carefully pack the dolls into my day-pack. "If there's no one home, just open the door and set them inside. Their doors probably won't be locked. They didn't use locks where they came from, and poor people don't fear burglars."

"But they're so valuable, especially to you."

"Not as valuable as the memory of giving them away."

"Don't you want to come with me? So you can see the girls' expressions when they get them?"

"Then they would know who they came from. That would spoil the fun. You're the only one who can do it."

"I'd love to, but why me? You have lots of friends."

"And any of them would be glad to do it. But they're not Native American. They don't understand how important giving and sharing are. They'd make a big thing out of it. I can trust you. You won't tell anyone."

The next day was the Saturday before Christmas, so there was no auction sale at the stockyards. I didn't think there'd be any work for me, but I showed up anyway, and the manager let me work for four hours cleaning barns. I was glad when he paid me before I went home.

As I headed down the hall toward the history room Monday afternoon, I recalled what I had been doing for the last three weeks. I had been waiting out in the hall until it was time for the bell to ring, then quietly slipping into my seat, hoping no one would notice me. I decided I wasn't doing that any more. I held my head up, walked confidently to Mr. Johnson's desk, and laid my ten dollar bill on it. It was probably my imagination, but I thought I detected a different look on the face of some of the boys—more like they would look at the opposite team in a football game, instead of a little dog they'd like to kick out of the way.

There were only two more days of school that week before we were out for Christmas vacation. Jose worked more hours than usual during vacation, but he had one day off, so we agreed to meet and spend the day climbing around in the rimrocks on the north side of town. On our way back, we went by a big machinery lot and stopped to look at the equipment. Jose started to laugh, and asked, "Remember when we were looking at those big mine trucks in Butte, back when we were in fifth grade?"

"And those boys started throwing rocks at us!"

"And we threw them back."

"They ran away, so we were the ones who got arrested, and you were sure you were going to get deported back to Mexico."

"Well," Jose answered, "we've learned a lot about city life and how to keep out of trouble since then."

"But we did have fun," I said.

"Speaking of fun, and keeping out of trouble, did you hear the announcement at school about the big party the Kiwanis Club is putting on at the Shrine New Year's Eve?"

"Yes," I said. "But I didn't pay much attention. There's always too much drinking at New Year's Eve parties."

"That's why the Kiwanians are putting it on, so all of us teenagers will have a place to go where there's no drinking."

"I'm not much good at dancing, except Indian dances."

"They might even have a couple of them," Jose answered. "They said they've got a top orchestra that plays every kind of music. Everything from hard rock to South American bomba. Maybe even African. Ought to be a lot of fun even if we just watch. You can't sit home on New Year's Eve."

"But I don't have anyone to take."

"You don't need a date. They said everyone should just come. No charge."

"Hmm, well, sounds pretty good. Okay. Do you want to come over to my place about a half hour before it starts? It's a long walk."

The orchestra had already started playing before Jose and I arrived. We found ourselves a table and sat drinking sodas. The gym was packed, and sure enough they had all kinds of music. I kept watching for Tobie, but I didn't see her. I hadn't really thought she would be there anyway.

Roger, Thomas, and Frank came walking by looking for girls to dance with. Roger stopped, stared at us, and exclaimed, "What in the world are you two doing here? Don't you know this is a non-drinking party? No drunken Indians allowed."

Frank followed up with, "How many drinks did you have before you came? Didn't they smell your breath before they let you in?"

Jose retorted, angrily, "That's why we came. We don't drink!"

"Maybe you don't," Thomas said, "But I'll bet Flint can't say that. All Indians drink!"

"There are Indians who are alcoholics," I said. "White eyes too! Trouble-makers who give the rest a bad name. But there are more Indians who are teetotalers than any other ethnic group."

Frank spoke up. "Ha! Yeah, right, whatever! You're trying to fool us with your fake statistics."

When they didn't move on Jose leaned over toward me, pointed at Thomas, and mumbled something that I couldn't understand. I finally caught on, and we both started to laugh.

"What are you saying? Speak up," Thomas said.

Jose didn't say a word. Just sat and grinned.

Thomas looked embarrassed and said, "All right, so I was bombed Saturday night. So what!" They made their way on down the row of tables.

We listened while the orchestra played two more songs. Then they started a fast Mexican tune, and Jose jumped up and was soon twirling across the floor with a pretty Mexican girl in a long fiesta dress. When he finished he brought two girls back to the table and wanted me to dance with one, but I told them I couldn't dance to that music. When the music switched to rock and roll, Jose came back to the table. I told him, "Boy, you sure do cut a rug on that Mexican music."

"You ought to see us at the Cinco d' Mayo."

"Cinco d' Mayo?"

"Yes. Fifth of May. The Mexican Independence Day celebration. You better come this year. We'll teach you the dances."

"Okay," I said. "If you'll go with me to the pow-wow and Indian rodeo on the Fourth of July."

About that time the orchestra broke into a Strauss waltz, and Tobie came out of the crowd walking toward our table. I was amazed to see her in a white dress with a full circle skirt. She looked gorgeous. Even her hair was under control. "Come on Flint, let's dance," she said as she reached out her hands for mine.

"I can't," I said. "I don't know how to waltz."

"I'll teach you. It's easy."

When I shook my head, she said, "This is my music. You can't deny me part of my culture. If this was a Cheyenne dance, you wouldn't want to miss out on it would you?"

"No."

"Well, this is my culture. Come on." She led me onto the dance floor and took both of my hands in hers. "Watch my feet. Left foot back. Right foot across. Then together. Left back, right across, together. Now follow me." After a few steps she put my right arm around her waist and continued to hold my left hand, and we were gliding across the floor together.

"What do you mean, your culture?" I asked. "How is the waltz part of your culture?"

"Finnish," she said. "I spent last year as an exchange student in Finland learning my culture. The Finns are like the Native Americans. They value the old ways. So they love the waltz."

"Finn? But I thought you were Apache and African!"

"That's my father's side. My mother is half Potawatami and half Finn."

"Oh! So you have four cultures. Two Native American and two others."

"Yes. And I value every one of them. I want to know all I can about everyone of them, and live them all thoroughly—and my fifth one too."

"Fifth one?"

"Yes. Urban American. It's yours too. We're going to live it so we better learn to love it. It's not all bad!"

When the music stopped, Tobie gave me a long, tight hug. Absolutely the best hug I ever had. I could feel my heart pounding. It pounded so hard I knew she must feel it, too, or hear it. She let go and I started to turn, to lead her toward the table, but she said "Wait." She took something out of her jacket pocket and slipped it into my pocket. "You can look at it later," she said. "They're starting again. A cowboy song! Isn't that a part of your culture?"

"Yes", I said. "I've worked a lot with the cattle on the rez. Lived on a ranch for a year, too. Won a couple of roping prizes. And I trained my dog, O'kohome as a cow dog—and a sled dog. But that's the past. I'm stuck in the city now."

We danced for a few minutes without saying a word, her head against my cheek. I don't know what steps we used. They just came naturally. She held me close and followed perfectly, every step. Suddenly she looked up at me. "Have you decided about your vision quest yet?"

"No. Grandfather and I were talking about it again this week. He wants to help me prepare. He thinks I should go on a vision quest before I go to the Beartooths. But I told him no one goes on a vision quest any more."

"Flint. Look at me. Do you think I'm crazy, getting involved in all my cultures?"

"No! Of course not! It's wonderful. But I . . ."

"You're afraid to get really involved in any culture, aren't you! You're afraid it will be taken away from you, so you don't want to prize it too highly."

"I guess you're right. But look at what's happened to . . .."

"Flint! You've got it all wrong. You need to get involved in every one of them. Everything. Each one makes your life a little richer. What's really in your heart can't ever be taken away. It'll always be there. Inside." The music stopped but she went on. "I may never see you again, but I'll never lose you. I'll always have you right here." She tapped herself over her heart. "And like it or not, you'll never be rid of me!" She winked and grinned as she turned, and walked away without ever looking back.

When I got back to the table, I reached into my pocket to see what Tobie had put there. It was a small, beautifully beaded doeskin pouch. The beaded design was the Morning Star—symbol of the Cheyenne nation. At the top, bottom, and both sides of the diamond shape were the four colors representing the four directions, the four seasons. Inside the diamond-shaped design was another small black symbol. I didn't know what it represented. Hardly an eagle or thunderbird, but perhaps some kind of long-winged bird. It had a line of black beads with one white bead near each end and one black bead above the line for a head, and two below the line for feet. A beadwork fringe decorated the bottom edge of the pouch. Attached to the top, but stuffed inside the pouch, was a buckskin thong, long enough to go around my neck and have the pouch hang to the middle of my chest. Obviously a "medicine bag." Inside was a note. "I didn't know what your spiritual symbol would be, so I used the symbol of your tribe. I can't go with you on your adventure, but perhaps this can. You'll know that in spirit I'm with you."

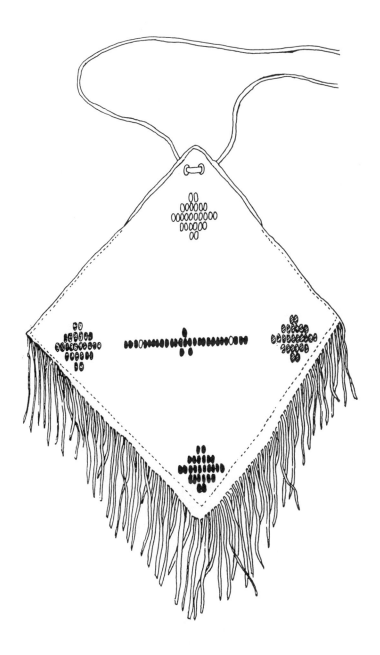

4
The Preparation

The first day of the new semester Jose and I found seats together in American History class. I tried to hold the seat on the other side of me, hoping Tobie would be willing to take it. But she never arrived. I wondered what happened to her. Was she not in school, or was she just not taking history this semester? When she wasn't in biology either, I remembered the last thing she had said to me: "I may never see you again." Could there be more meaning to that statement than I thought?

Roger and Jose were the only students I knew in woodworking class. Jose had signed up for the class when I told him I was taking it. Roger just ignored me. The shop teacher described several different projects that students could do. "For those of you who weren't in the fall class, I'll have to check you out on basic skills. We'll do a couple of simple projects, then you can pick your own."

I went to him after class and asked if I could make a bow and some arrows.

"So you're the one," he said. "Tobie said you had worked on a ranch so you've probably done some basic carpentry work. Is that right?"

"Well, yes, my dad ran a ranch for a year. And then he worked with the tribal herd till he took the job here in Billings this fall. He often had to make what he needed and I helped him."

"A rancher has to be able to do a little of everything. Once I've checked you on some basic skills, and explained our procedures, then you can get started on your bow. Lemonwood works well. I'll see what else we have. I have plans for the new compound bows that are the best for hunting."

"No." I said. "I'd rather have the recurve bow, the old Indian type." I explained what I was going to do next fall. "I want to do everything the old Native American way as much as possible. I think I'll need a toboggan too. I'll have to take more stuff than I can carry, and a travois won't work well on narrow mountain trails. I've trained my dog to help me pull it. Indians invented the toboggan, didn't they?"

"Yes, but a loaded toboggan would be almost impossible for you to pull on a bare trail without any snow. Besides, if you dragged it over those rough, rocky Beartooth trails, the bottom would be so roughed up it would hardly slide on the snow when it came. What you need is a dog sled, like the Athabascans use in Alaska. We can put a strip of hard plastic along the bottom of the runners, and it will slide well on both bare ground and snow. I have some plans in my files."

Both archery class and woodworking went well that first week. I found a couple of friendly people in each class, and began to feel better about school. I wanted to find Tobie and thank her for recommending those classes, but I watched the halls all week, and never saw her. Monday, after school, I hurried to the university library, but she never did show up for our exercise and study sessions. I asked the girls she had sat with in history last semester, but no one knew why she wasn't in school. I thought of going to her home, but no one seemed to know where she lived. She had always been somewhat of a mystery, and now her disappearance was even more of one.

About three weeks later the letter came in the mail. I was sitting on my bed, the only place I had to do my homework, and was just about to put my books away when my Mother said, "A letter came today, addressed to you with no sender's name, just a printed return address on it. It's probably just an ad. It's on the fridge."

The address on the envelope was some camp in Oregon. Mom was probably right. I didn't know anyone out there. But I tore the end off the envelope and pulled out the letter. It was signed "Tobie." My heart jumped a couple of beats and I anxiously read the letter.

Flint,

I'm sitting here on a rainy Sunday afternoon, getting ready to take on my homework and all the practical matters I didn't have time for all week. Somehow I just couldn't start until I scratched out a note to you. I've been snowshoeing, and every time I get out in the snow I can't help thinking of you. Whether it's light fluffy powder that even my snowshoes sink into, or icy snow that crunches with every step, I think of you alongside of me, pointing out tracks.

I know you must have wondered what happened to me. I'm on my way to Peru, or I will be soon. Last fall, I applied for a grant to attend a conference and a three-month work session sponsored by the Alliance for Indigenous Peoples. Representatives from several Canadian and U.S. tribes are going down to work with the Native Indians of Peru. Native people from several Asian and African nations will be there too. We'll discuss mutual problems and how we can help each other. They wanted one high school student, someone who could build relationships with Peruvian teenagers and open up discussions with them. I applied for the grant, but I didn't tell anyone because I knew there were thousands of other applicants. When my acceptance came, I hopped on a plane to Arizona to spend two weeks with my grandfather to discuss ideas with him before coming to Oregon for a three-week training session. How great it would be if you were going, to add another teenage voice!

We have the weekend free, but the trip is coming up so quickly. It's taking my breath away. So much going on here. So much to learn. And classes. Such intensity in all my new friendships. Yet a large part of me doesn't want to leave. Who else could I talk to but you. You are the one who understands my adventurous spirit, and sympathizes with my Native side that loves this soil and this land. You'd know the pangs in my heart for the months I will be separated from it. You and I, we who are born to the land, have that delicate, sharp feeling of not just living in a place, but of coming to know it—like one does a dear friend. We and the land have come to an appreciation of one another. The land guides us, and I know it forgives my two-legged stumblings.

There is so much to do. But I simply can't spend it inside four walls. I had to get out where I could commune with the land and nature. So yesterday I went snowshoeing alone, wandered through the untouched snow. What a joy to be out where there were no other humans. The trees spoke plenty. A raven watched my progress, bemused. I thought what huge tracks my snowshoes left. I wondered what you would say about those huge Tobie tracks. Would you know they were Tobie tracks by the way I walked?

I borrowed the snowshoes. Then I started last week to make some snowshoes of my own. They're pretty rough, but who needs everything perfect? Maybe they'll be good enough for you to use in the Beartooths if you can't borrow better ones.

I went snowshoeing again this afternoon, but with a friend. We examined the tracks of winter animals: squirrel, a bird. Small stories whispered in the snow. Most of the tracks my friend knew. The ones that he did not, I knew that you would. And you could tell me the stories that they told you. Some of them I even asked you about in my head, but received no answer. You must have been challenging me to observe for myself. The fog moved in and the way became dim before we got back. There is only a light place in the west to tell me that I must be moving on to practical matters. I wonder what color the sky is in Montana tonight.

> Warm tea, cozy blankets,
> Tobie

I started to put the letter back in the envelope when I discovered that inside was another smaller envelope sealed tightly with tape. On it was written, "Save this. Do not open until the day of your vision quest." I hesitated. I really wanted to open it right away. But I didn't. I put it in my pocket. Then I went to the stove and made myself a cup of warm tea. Needless to say, I was already dreaming of Tobie long before I went to sleep.

The next day, after school, I went to the big supermarket where they had all kinds of candy, nuts and granola in bins. I put three Hershey's Kisses, three of the bigger Hershey's Hugs, and three unpitted dates in a sack. When I took them to the cashier she asked, "Is that all?"

"Yes, unless you happen to have a real small box I could mail these in."

She laughed and said, "I think I saw one under here." She rummaged around under the counter and came up with a box just the size of a small envelope. I put the candy and dates in it and she laughed again. "I suppose now you need a valentine to put in there."

"Something like that. Just a little piece of paper. Guess I'll have to go home and dig one out."

She pulled a few inches of tape out of her adding machine and handed me a ball point pen along with it. "Will this do?"

"Sure will." I wrote on the tape, "Take this with you. When you are in Peru and are a little lonely, and wish you had a date, take one. Then take a hug. Savor it slowly as you think of someone you would like to share it with. If you think the kisses are inappropriate, remember that you can always return a kiss. When you get back you can return it—to someone—somewhere—sometime—maybe!"

I didn't sign the note, or put any return address on the box. I remembered Tobie and the dolls and knew it would be more fun to send it without a signature. As I taped the box shut, I realized that I didn't even know Tobie's last name! I just addressed it to "Tobie" using the name and address of the camp from the envelope she had sent.

In the next six weeks I completed my bow and made a lot of progress on my sled. Roger came over and watched me for a few minutes and asked, "Are you going to use this in the Beartooths next fall?"

"Yes," I said.

"I saw that bow you made. It's a beauty! You really are serious, aren't you? You're really going to do it!"

"I sure am. You can bet on it."

"I already did," Roger said with a laugh. He looked the sled over carefully. Knowing his attitude toward me last fall, I expected a lot of criticism. But he seemed genuinely interested and started asking

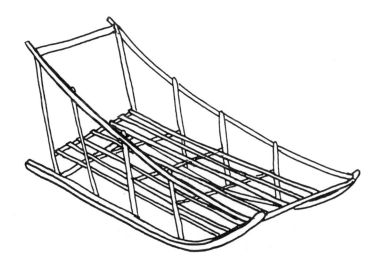

questions about it. I explained that I was making the runners so they would only keep the sled about three inches from the ground. They would slide easily over packed snow, or even bare ground or tundra. But if there was deep powder snow, the bottom of the sled itself would ride on it like a toboggan. I showed him how it was all put together with rawhide, instead of nails and screws. With all the twisting and bouncing over rough country, screws eventually work out, but the rawhide gives, and it can last for years.

"Are you doing some of this stuff at home, too?" Roger asked.

I still didn't trust his attitude. I remembered how he ridiculed everything I said in history class. But finally I told him, "Grandfather Wolf Runner got a ride up to Billings with Henry Knows-His-Horses a week ago. He brought some deer hides, and some deer brains that he froze last fall. We put wood ashes on the hides and buried them to loosen the hair. Yesterday, we dug them up and started scraping the hair off. In a couple of days we'll start rubbing in the brains to tan them; then we'll smoke the buckskins so when they get wet, and then dry out, they will stay soft."

"What are you going to do with them?"

"Mom's going to help me make a buckskin shirt and leggings. I've always wanted some. Sis says she'll bead them and make me some mittens. I told her I didn't need beadwork on a shirt to wear in the Beartooths, but she says I'll feel more like a warrior. I'm going to have a real parka, too. Mom went down to Goodwill and bought three old worn-out fur coats. She's going to use the good parts of the fur to make me a good warm parka."

"What are you going to sleep in? A regular sleeping bag? It better be a good down one. It'll be awful cold up there before you come home. Way below zero, I'll bet."

"I guess I'll have to try to get a good one," I said. "What I really should have is a buffalo robe, but there's nowhere to get one. It would cost a fortune if I tried to buy one. The Crows have some buffalo, but the Cheyennes don't."

A couple of weeks later in woodshop, I was busy sanding the side rails of the dog sled when Roger laid down the project he was working on and walked over. He stood and watched for a few minutes, studying the sled. I didn't look up. I was determined to ignore him if he started making snide remarks about it.

"Fantastic!" he said. "I can't believe there is so much detail work in making a dog sled. It's beautiful."

"Well, fair at least. I try to work up to the standard of the old culture; but they put their lives into it. I can't quite qualify, but I try."

Roger grinned. "Two months ago I'd have laughed at that statement. But you got me interested. I've been studying. I went down to the Native American craft exhibit that's at the Heritage Center this week. I can't believe the fine detail work that went into that stuff, everything from the baskets to the headdresses."

I agreed with him. "I think I'm doing great, till I go look at the old stuff. I can't match it. But what I can make will serve my purposes in the Beartooths."

"Well, you've convinced me. You even got me interested enough to do some research in the library. I was completely wrong about you and your people. I guess you did know what you were talking about when you claimed that more than half of the world's food supply came from the American Indians. And I found out the Indians do have the biggest percent of non-drinkers."

Roger helped me turn the sled around so I could work on the other side. "It's lighter than I expected," he said. "Shouldn't be too hard to pull."

I told him, "I have a dog that I trained to pull a sled when he was a pup. I call him O'kohome. That's Cheyenne for coyote. He's half coyote, but I wish he was half wolf instead, because wolves are bigger and tougher. They can pull a heavier load. But he'll be a help pulling it, and he'll keep my feet warm at night."

"Maybe I can get you some help on that. I've got an uncle who worked out in the bush of Alaska for about six years. Loves that kind of life. Brought back all kinds of stuff. I was telling him about how you are going up to live alone in that wilderness area. He says he'd like to meet you. He's got half a dozen tanned caribou hides he's been planning to give away, taking up space in his garage. He says caribou is the warmest thing there is cause every hair is hollow to give it extra insulation. Think you could use them?"

"Boy, could I! Might be even better than buffalo robes to keep me from freezing to death, on those two-dog nights when even the thermometer freezes up. And come to think of it, that's just as traditional Cheyenne as buffalo robes, if you go back far enough. Three hundred years ago the Cheyenne lived north of the Great Lakes, and their meat was caribou, not buffalo."

We talked about that for a minute, then Roger made another offer. "My uncle has some fur boots too. A double layer of fur with sealskin on the outside and sheepskin on the inside. They are like regular mukluks except they've got rubber boot soles added to give you traction on the ice. Says he hasn't used 'em in years."

"Gee, if they fit I could sure use them. I asked Mom if she could make me some high top fur moccasins, but she said she couldn't make them waterproof. And she says you shouldn't wear mukluks unless you grew up in them. Too much danger of falling."

"Good. I'll load them and the hides in my pickup and bring them over to your place. How about Saturday?"

"Saturday afternoon would be great. I work at the stockyards Saturday mornings."

By the end of the school year I had finished making nearly everything I would need except some of my arrows. I wanted to take about forty because I wouldn't have the tools or the right wood to make more up in the Beartooths. I was being especially particular about my arrows because I would have to depend on them for most of my food. For some I bought the razor sharp steel arrowheads that are popular for big game. Others with blunt tips like we used in archery class would be good for birds and maybe squirrels.

When we moved to Billings I brought several pieces of flint from the big rock above Lame Deer where my ancestors collected theirs. When I was a little kid I spent a lot of time up there. I practiced making flint arrowheads, but I was still no expert. I got the flint rocks out and spent several evenings trying, until I thought I had one arrowhead as good as

I could make it. I was especially careful with the feathers I put on that arrow. I wanted it to be perfect.

I showed the flint-headed arrow to Grandfather. He looked it over very carefully and said, "That one's good enough to carry the spirit of your ancestors. We'll call it your spirit arrow. We'll take the arrow into the sweat bath we use to get you ready for your vision quest, and make it a part of the ceremony."

I was still a little hesitant about the idea of a vision quest. I wasn't afraid of fasting four days, but I guess I just wasn't that spiritual in my daily life, as the Cheyenne used to be. Maybe I wasn't deserving enough to have a vision. But I didn't interrupt Grandfather to argue the point.

"You'll need your good arrows to get your meat," he said, "but don't be spending all your time hunting. Remember, the animals are your friends. Enjoy them. They are kindred spirits. And don't ever kill more than is necessary for food. Remember, if you don't show your appreciation or if you waste any part of an animal you catch, the next one won't offer his life for you." I had already realized the animals would be my only companions. This was even more reason why every arrow should be perfect. The arrow must fly true and kill—never leaving a crippled animal.

Grandfather went on, emphasizing the importance of thanking the spirit for every animal killed. "Remember there's spirit in everything," he said. "Carry your spirit arrow with you. It will remind you not to forget your traditions."

I showed the arrows I had finished to my archery instructor and he told me, "With those arrows and the skill you have developed, you should have no difficulty getting plenty of game."

"If it stands still," I said.

He picked up the arrow with the stone arrowhead and exclaimed, "This is a beauty. Did you make the arrowhead?"

"Uh-huh. That's my 'spirit arrow'. Some of the old Cheyennes had spirit arrows that they never used except in defense of their people. They said they couldn't lose a battle if they used one. I'll keep it in my quiver to feel like a real Cheyenne warrior." Then I laughed as I added, "Might even save my life."

He laughed with me, then commented, "Well, if you need it, that one will probably kill a deer as well as any you have—but don't lose it!"

There was just one thing I was making that contained modern materials the old Cheyenne didn't have—a small survival kit. I showed it to Jose and Roger. In it I had a pocket lighter and a candle. "If you're out in a rain or a snowstorm, you can't get a fire started with a lighter or a match," I told them. "But with a candle you can keep a flame going long enough to get one started." I also had a compass with a mirror on the back for signaling, a scratch pad and a stub of a pencil, some fish line and a couple of fish hooks, and some fine copper wire for making rabbit snares.

"I thought you were supposed to use sinew for that," Jose said.

"Yes, but the copper wire works better. For my survival kit I don't mind using the modern stuff. You couldn't get this in the old days either," I said as I unfolded my space blanket. It was made from foil to reflect body heat and was big enough to wrap up in.

"You think that'll keep you warm in a blizzard?" Jose asked.

"I'm not going to be out in a blizzard. But I can dig into a snowdrift and make a snow cave if I have to. Snow is good insulation."

Jose picked up the space blanket. "Hmmm, only a couple of ounces. I don't think it'll keep you very warm."

"Better than nothing. It's just for emergencies. I don't plan on any emergencies, but you never know."

"I think I'll make one of those emergency kits," Roger said, "and take it with me when I go hiking this summer."

"Don't leave camp without it," I told him. "Those fifteen minutes you planned could turn into three days."

The afternoon of the last Saturday before school was out, a little old Yupik Eskimo woman knocked at our door. "Are you Flint?" she asked.

"Yes. That's me."

"Then this must be yours." She pulled something out of her shopping bag and handed it to me. It was a fur hat, the kind with ear flaps that can be tied under your chin when it's cold. As I looked it over she explained, "I moved to Billings right after Christmas, and the house I moved into was like a garbage heap. This high school girl who lived down the block came down and helped me clean up the house and move in. I had a whole bunch of beaver skins with me from Alaska, and I was making beaver hats to sell. They were only one layer of fur, with cloth inside. This girl paid me to make one for her, with fur on the inside and outside. She said she'd pick it up in March or April, but she never showed up. Yesterday, I got a letter from her that said she was living with a family who needs help. The father disappeared, the mother was injured, and she didn't want to leave till the mother was well. She asked me to bring this hat to you right away because she thought you might be leaving when school was out."

"What was her name?"

"She just signed the letter, 'The girl who helped you move in'."

"Did you look at the postmark to see where it was from?"

"The stamp was from Peru."

A ranger at the U.S. Forest Service office in Billings showed me maps of the Beartooth Wilderness Area, and suggested that I follow the Stillwater River and camp at Sioux Charlie Lake. I told him that I wanted to go higher into an area away from the trails.

"It would be too hard to get out in winter if you got injured or needed help," he said. "I wouldn't take the chance."

There was only one four-day weekend between school and the beginning of the Upward Bound project at the university. Roger offered to take me up to the Beartooth Mountains to look for a good location, and Jose went along. Roger borrowed three sleeping bags and a backpack tent.

We parked at the Woodbine campground, then took our packs and hiked west, up the river to Sioux Charlie Lake. A creek ran into the lake from a valley on the south side that apparently had no marked trail leading in. "Let's try it," I said. After a steep climb and a long cross-country haul over some downed timber in the dense lodgepole pine forest, we followed some old deer trails up the valley to a big beaver dam. Above the beaver pond was a swampy area where two cow moose and a calf grazed. We took the long way around them. Jose wanted to get a closer look, but I told him there's nothing more dangerous than a moose who wants to keep you away from her calf.

Spreading out above the swamp was a small meadow. Roger and Jose walked over to a large boulder on the east side of the meadow, took off their packs, and plopped down on the pine needles under a big tree. "Let's camp here tonight," Jose said. "I'm worn out."

"And that boulder will give us a good wind break if that breeze turns into a storm," Roger said.

"This might be a good starting campsite when I come up in September," I told them. "It might take me two days to get here pulling the sled, but this will be a good destination. You two will know where it is and maybe you can come up to spend a weekend before snow flies."

"Will you be staying in one spot?" Jose asked.

"I'll have to set up a permanent camp, then hike and explore from there," I said, "because I'll have a lot more stuff than I can carry. Anyway, I'm doing it the old Cheyenne way. Of course, I'll be traveling around a lot, hunting. It will be like how the Cheyenne hunted buffalo. I want to explore the whole area, and maybe climb a couple of mountains. The Cheyenne always settled in at a permanent base camp before snow came, and I'll have to do that, too."

The next morning we decided to hike on up the valley and explore a little. About a quarter of a mile up at the far end of the meadow was another big rock with a big tree beside it. "I think this would be a better campsite for me," I told them. "It's closer to the stream that feeds into the beaver dam. I don't want to get my drinking water from that swampy area above the beaver pond. If I find a better permanent location, it shouldn't be too far away. If I move, I'll leave a note telling you how to find it."

"In picture writing, I suppose," Jose said. We all laughed.

"There's even a good place to leave your message," Roger said, pointing to a flat rock that sat on top of the big boulder. "Leave it under that rock."

"I think there's already a message here," Jose said. "Aren't those grizzly claw marks?" He pointed to some big gouges in the bark of the tree about a foot above my head. "Are you sure you want to camp here?"

I told him, "It's a message all right. It means that a bear is marking his territory. He might be a grizzly, but not a very big one, and the marks are old. He's probably long gone." I studied the claw marks again and added. "But I might decide to camp on up the valley somewhere."

Jose pulled out the Forest Service map and started studying it.

Roger asked, "Is there a name for this valley?"

"Just a crooked line for the stream," Jose said.

"Well, I'm calling it Grizzly Valley," Roger decided. "Write it in."

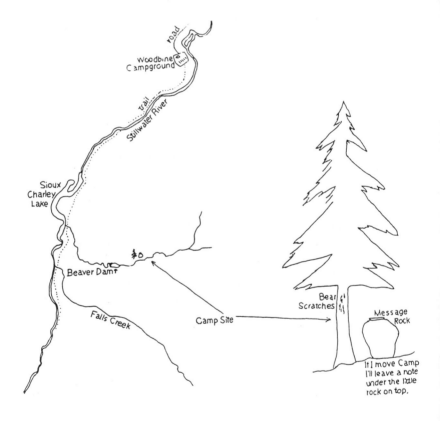

When we got home, I drew a map of the route to my planned campsite for my parents, so that while I was on my venture, they would feel a little more comfortable; they would know exactly where I was. I even added a picture of the tree with the bear scratches on it, the big rock beside it, and the message rock on top. I marked it Grizzly Valley. Before I gave the map to Mom, I took it down to the drugstore and made two copies. One was for Roger and one was for Jose. I hoped to encourage them to come visit me.

The Upward Bound project that Tobie had suggested I sign up for kept me so busy most of the summer that I didn't have time to think about anything else. Those classes really encouraged me to consider college more seriously, and they made me feel more secure about trying it. I remembered that Tobie had given me a college application form that I never got around to filling out. When the Upward Bound director brought out a stack of college application forms, I hunted for one for the University of Arizona, where Tobie had said she was going; I filled it out. I should have filled out some others, but the program was ending, and after we moved out of the dormitory I didn't have time to think about school. I was too busy trying to get ready for my time in the Beartooths. I only had three weeks.

They gave us three days off for the Fourth of July. I went to the Cheyenne pow-wow in Lame Deer. Tobie had said she wanted to go to it, but I hadn't heard a thing from her. I wondered if she was still in Peru.

I entered the Fancy Dance contest for men, thinking that if I could win one of the prizes it would give me money enough to buy the canvas for a small tipi. But I didn't have a chance. Most of the contestants had been practicing every week, all year round. But I did have fun dancing. I would have entered the roping competition at the rodeo, but I didn't have a horse.

Jose came down for the last evening of the pow-wow. I wanted him to see all the different kinds of dances, and to be there for the feast. Most of the visitors were gone by midnight and didn't even know about the feast. After the feast, they had the last give-away. The announcer called out the name of each family who wanted to give gifts. Then, he announced the names of the people who were to come forward and receive them. Jose could hardly believe the number of things that people gave away. They parted with dozens and dozens of blankets, lots of beadwork, Native American jewelry, and two saddle horses.

"The Henry Knows-His-Horses family," the announcer sang out. He turned to Henry and then announced, "A tipi for Flint Red Coyote."

I couldn't believe my ears. Jose went up with me to get it. Henry told me, "It's too small for our family, but it's just right for one or two people. Everything's here, even a liner for extra warmth. Everything is here except the poles."

5

The Sweat Lodge Ceremony

When the Upward Bound project was over, I spent a couple of days with my parents and then caught a ride down to the reservation. I wanted to stay with Grandfather Wolf Runner while I prepared myself for my challenge and collect the things I would need.

Last December, when I first decided to go on my challenge, Grandfather said that in the old days a young warrior usually didn't go on a challenge to prove his courage and manhood until after he had gone on a vision quest and learned who his spirit helper was. I told him that I didn't need to go on a vision quest. I said, "They were all right for your generation and before, but no one believes in them anymore. Very few people even consider going on a vision quest, and if they do, usually don't have a vision."

Grandfather's answer had been, "Perhaps they didn't have visions because their prayers and their plans were too selfish. Pray always for the good of your people, or even all of mankind. For yourself, ask for purity, for strength, for endurance, for oneness with all people and with all of nature."

If that was what was needed, I really hadn't been prepared for it then. But now that I had spent six months preparing for my challenge and it was getting closer, I began to think that if I was really doing things the old way, really trying to experience the old culture, a vision quest needed to be a part of it. I went to Grandfather and asked if he thought we could squeeze one in before I was to leave.

"That is something you cannot rush," he said. "It requires a lot of spiritual preparation. Look at me." He sat for some time, looking deeply into my eyes, and finally spoke. "No, you are not ready. It is doubtful that you could be ready for a vision quest before you go on your challenge. But after you get up there and have spent some time alone in the wilderness, after you have had time to let your spirit and mind become one with the natural world, then you may be ready. If you do go on a quest, you must be ready to accept whatever vision you have, because it will be a message from the Creator, the right message for you, and a guide for your life. I will help you prepare for your quest before you go on your challenge. One thing you can do now is make yourself a medicine pouch to wear around your neck. Then you can put things in it that will remind you of your vision and help to give you spiritual power throughout your life."

"I already have one. Tobie made it for me." I pulled it from inside my shirt and showed it to him.

"This is good," he said, surprised. "And it even has the Morning Star, the symbol of the Cheyenne! Now let's see. The main thing we should do to get you ready for both your challenge and your vision quest is to have a sweat for you. As I'm sure you know, the sweat lodge ceremony is one of the things that our people haven't lost. Many of us still use it when we're facing a serious problem and feel the need for help. It will give you a feeling of spiritual security. Maybe you'd prefer to just call it self-assurance."

I wanted to be ready for the sweat lodge and my quest, but I had many other things to do before going on my challenge in two weeks. I headed out to dig wild turnips and cattail roots and pick chokecherries and rose hips. I dried all of them along with many tomatoes. Two neighbors offered me their leftover jerky from last year's deer hunting. They would be hunting again soon and make more. I made some jerky from beef also, but I ground it, along with most of my dried chokecherries, to make pemmican.

Finally I thought I had prepared enough food to last me three or four weeks. I was confident that during my first month in the Beartooth Mountains I would find plenty of meat and wild berries to last me a couple of months. I'd save as much as possible of the stuff I had dried, to use during the last month when I might get snowed in. Most of the plants would be gone then, and many of the animals would be hibernating.

One day, not long before I was to leave, Grandfather suggested that we go for a walk in the forest up beyond the cliffs south of Lame Deer. We walked for a long time without saying a word. The only sounds were the songs of the birds and the buzzing of the insects. Finally Grandfather asked, "Do you think you are ready, physically, mentally, and spiritually for your challenge and vision quest?"

I looked into Grandfather's eyes and I could see in them the depth of his wisdom, and understanding. And I knew that he could see in me any weakness, or hesitancy. I knew that I could never come back and pretend I had had a vision. He would know without a doubt. But I said without hesitancy, "Yes, Grandfather, I'm ready for my challenge. All spring I built my strength and studied. Lately I have been praying, getting ready for my quest."

It seemed he looked deep into my eyes forever as he listened to the sounds of nature all around us. I heard the song of a meadow lark and the cry of a hawk. I wondered if they were speaking to him. Finally he put his hand on my shoulder and said, "You are ready. Three days from now, the day before you leave for the wilderness, we will have the Sweat Lodge ceremony. Are there any special people you would like to have with you?"

"Well Dad, and Uncle David, and Henry Knows-His-Horses. Do they have to be Cheyenne?"

"Not if they'll take it seriously and participate. Remember that everything must be done with reverence, for we are asking God, the Great Spirit, to give you help and guidance."

"How about Jose? You met him when you were in Billings. And Roger. Roger's taking me up to the Beartooths. I'm sure neither of them has ever had a sweat, and I'm sure they'd both like to learn about it."

"Good. You're leaving Saturday aren't you? Give them a call to see if they can come down a day early in time for the sweat Friday afternoon. We'll put up my tipi for the three of you to sleep in."

"They'll like that."

There was a brush frame for a sweat lodge near the west bank of Lame Deer Creek facing east. It had been ceremonially blessed by a medicine man, so was ready for use. We covered it with canvas and quilts to keep the steam in, and we set up the tipi nearby. Jose, Roger, and I gathered and cut wood and built a hot fire several yards in front of the entrance to the sweat lodge. We hunted for rocks to heat in it while Grandfather checked to see that we didn't have any rocks from the creek. "Creek rocks might have enough moisture in them to explode when they get hot."

Grandmother and Mrs. Knows-His-Horses drove up in a pickup, and Grandmother said, "Get that big can of water and the dipper out of the back, and be sure everyone drinks plenty before they go in. We don't want anybody passing out in there." As soon as we had unloaded, they drove away. Henry Knows-His-Horses arrived, bringing two other men with him.

As an eagle flew over us and climbed high into the sky, Grandfather looked at the group gathered and said, "Do not go in unless you intend to do it reverently, this purification ceremony is a sacred event. Regardless of what He is called in your language, God, Ma'heo'o, Wakan Tonka, Manitou, Jehovah, we are calling on the Creator, the Great Father of all people, to give Flint guidance and strength throughout this ceremony, his vision quest, and his challenge. Flint will be dedicating his body, his mind, and his soul to the service of his people, just like the great Cheyenne profit, Sweet Medicine, and even Christ himself, who went into the wilderness to seek guidance. We must be surrounded only by pure thoughts. We have to be humble because the fire represents the great power of the Creator, and the steam that rises around us represents His lasting strength and guidance with which He surrounds us. We must show reverence, not only for the

Father above us, but for the Earth Mother under our feet, who provides for all of our needs. Are you all prepared for this?"

We all nodded our heads.

We watched as Henry Knows-His-Horses put more wood on the fire, with the sticks pointing from the center toward the four directions. Then he put the rocks on the fire and we waited until they were turning red with the heat. We left our clothes outside and Grandfather talked in a hushed tone as he told us, "Bend you bodies low as you enter this lodge to show your humility in the presence of the Great Father, who is everything."

I stooped beneath the low roof, but I felt as if I was almost floating—as if my feet were hardly touching the ground. We all sat in a circle around the edges of the sweat lodge. One rock was brought in and placed in the center of the pit. It glowed red in the dim light inside.

Other rocks were placed around it in the four directions, then others were piled on.

When the canvas was pulled down to cover the door, it was almost totally dark inside. Grandfather took some sweet grass and tossed it onto the hot rocks, filling the air with its aroma. Then he poured water over them and clouds of steam rose around us. Henry Knows-His-Horses began beating a slow, steady rhythm on his drum. We sat for a time, listening to the drum, relaxing our bodies and minds, until we were all sweating well. I closed my eyes. A picture of Tobie flashed through my mind. I wished she could share this experience, share these thoughts. She was the one person I knew who would participate wholeheartedly, and appreciate every minute of it.

The fourth time Grandfather poured water on the rocks, the steam became so thick and hot that we had to lean forward so our faces were nearly to the ground, where there was cooler air to breathe.

A man sang a sacred song, asking that our minds and our souls be purified as the sweat cleansed our bodies inside and out. I wished that Jose and Roger could understand the Cheyenne words, but I was sure they must feel their spirits being lifted, like the eagle that we had watched climbing into the sky. As I felt the strength enter my body, I knew that the spirit would guide me throughout my challenge, and I longed for the day that I could go on my quest for a vision that would shape my life.

Grandfather began talking of our close relationship with Mother Earth, and with our Creator. He also spoke of the importance of caring for our fellow men, and everything in nature, and how we should guard the rights and welfare of each. He allowed plenty of time for thought, and for anyone else to express his own ideas. Then there was time for each person who wished to offer a prayer for my well being, safety, and good judgment during the next three months. Grandfather handed me my 'spirit arrow', and said, "Let this remind you that our spirits are with you."

As we sat silently and listened to the slow, steady rhythm of the drum, I realized the magnitude of the task before me, of the possible difficulty of what I would have to do, and of the importance of living up to the expectations of my friends. But I also felt a serenity that I hadn't had before, a great confidence in my own ability, in the strength that nature could provide.

Grandfather looked at the three of us and said that he was pleased that the other two had also kept their spirits in harmony with the ceremony. He said that good would come from this for all of us. He raised the canvas door and said a last prayer before the drumbeat ceased. We followed him out into the sunshine, our faces glowing and our bodies dripping with sweat.

I motioned for my friends to follow as I made a dash for and dived into the cool water of Lame Deer Creek. Laughing and shouting, we splashed water at each other, then returned to the sweat lodge to dress.

6

Alone

The next morning, we loaded everything I was taking with me to the Beartooth Mountains into the back of Roger's pickup and put the dog sled on top. I harnessed my dog, O'kohome, in the middle to make sure he couldn't get to the edge and try to jump out, since he wasn't used to riding in a pickup.

We were about to climb in when Grandfather came out of the house carrying a stick about four feet long. He looked at all the stuff we had loaded into the pickup and shook his head. Then he asked me, "How are you getting back home when you come out of the Beartooths? Is someone picking you up?"

"I am," Roger told him.

"How are you going to know when to go after him?"

"We have it all arranged. I'll be at the Woodbine trailhead the afternoon of December fifteenth, three months from now. Ten days before Christmas."

Grandfather looked at me, "And how are you going to know when that is? Are you carrying a white man's calendar? Or do you expect the Christmas star to shine for you—as they tell us it did for the wise men?"

"I'm not that wise," I said. "I'm taking a little notebook. Thought I'd keep a sort of a journal."

"And you're positive you'll write in it every day."

"Well I—Maybe I'd be wise to take a calendar, too."

"Doesn't your watch tell you the date?" Roger asked. "I assumed it did."

"I don't have a watch."

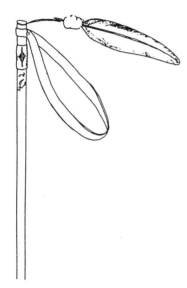

Roger looked shocked. He looked down at his watch, then at me, and back at his watch—as if he thought I should have it.

Grandfather reached out and handed me the long stick he was carrying. "This'll do it," he said.

I examined the stick. A leather loop at the top made it look a lot like a cross-country ski pole, except it was a little bigger around. Above the leather loop, attached by a short thong, was a large eagle feather, then there was a buckskin band decorated with porcupine quill work. Below that were some carved, picture-writing symbols. I slipped my hand through the loop and pushed as I would with a ski pole. "This would make a great hiking staff," I said. "I really should carry one, but this is much too valuable."

"Take it and use it. You'll need it for all those mountain trails you'll be climbing. But take good care of it. It's my coup stick. My grandfather made it for me when I became a warrior. Now it's yours."

"A coup stick! I've heard of them. All the warriors used to have one, didn't they? I can't believe it. You had one? Weren't you supposed to carve something on it whenever you counted coup? I thought they were shorter than this."

"Most of them were. I guess my grandfather thought I was going to count coup many times. Like the Crow Chief Plenty Coups, maybe. But by the time I was your age the enemy was no longer the Blackfeet or the Crow. You can't count coup on the U.S. government!"

I raised the coup stick and held it out in front of me. I imagined myself riding my pinto through the door of the Bureau of Indian Affairs, giving a great whoop as I touched the head honcho with my coup stick, and riding away as he tore up the latest batch of regulations. Roger's strange look brought me back to reality and I lowered the stick. "But—but why haven't I ever seen it?"

"I've kept it hidden, so no one could confiscate it for some museum."

"Could they do that?"

"Sixty years ago they could do anything."

"But why are you giving it to me?"

"Because I can't count coup any more. If you complete the three months alone in the wilderness and come out with your head up, that will be an accomplishment worthy of a warrior—a brave deed that deserves honor. That's what a coup is. Choose a symbol to represent it and carve it. You should also add the symbol that will record your vision if you have one."

I knew this must be Grandfather's most prized possession. I hesitated to accept it, but finally said, "This is a great honor. It will be an inspiration every day I'm up there. It will keep me from getting discouraged . . . but what does it have to do with the date I'm coming home? How is this going to tell me when Roger is coming to pick me up?"

"Remember that every day you stay up there is an accomplishment, a small honor worthy of recording. There is a ridge down the back of the coup stick. Every morning when you get up, take your knife and make a notch in that ridge. Leave a space between the months and it will be easier to count the days. When you have fifteen notches for December, you'll know that it's time to be back. . . Go! and let the Great Father go with you and guide you!"

It was well into the afternoon when we finally arrived at the Woodbine trailhead. "I hope you have that fur parka where you can get it easy," Jose said. "Look at those black clouds gathering. Looks like it could pour any minute."

"You better not waste any time getting a lot of firewood cut," Roger said. "You've got to be ready for winter. It could snow any day now. And you know how time flies."

"In Mexico, we said 'Time walks,' " Jose said. "We don't worry quite so much."

"Grandfather says 'time is here,'" I told them. "He says don't worry about tomorrow. Make today good and tomorrow will be good."

"Maybe so," Roger said, "but today won't be very good if we don't get the sled loaded before that storm hits."

We put my backpack in the front of the sled. I spread the tipi over my big bag of food and the caribou hides to keep them dry. As we fastened the two ropes to the front and attached the short one to O'kohome's harness, it started to sprinkle.

"Better dig out that parka. It's gonna be cold," Roger told me. "I hope you have a raincoat, too."

"A rain suit, it, and the little emergency kit I made, are my two concessions to modern convenience." I dug into my pack and had barely gotten the rain suit on when the rain started coming down by the bucketful.

"Better get in the car and wait it out," Roger shouted.

"No, I've got to get going." As Jose and Roger dashed for the car, I tied the longer rope around my waist, gave them a wave, and started up the trail. I turned and shouted, "Be sure and come up for a weekend."

"We'll try. If I can get off work."

O'kohome pulled hard in spite of the rain in his face. I think he was as glad as I was to be out on the trail. Not even a drenching rain could dampen my spirits on this, the first day of my adventure.

Even with the plastic covered runners, pulling that sled over the rough trail was certainly not easy. It wasn't a half hour before the rain ended suddenly and the sun came out. Now I was getting soaked with sweat instead of rain. I had to stop and take my rainsuit off. As we went west up the Stillwater River, there was a continual series of rapids and falls that I enjoyed during our frequent rest stops. The river certainly didn't live up to its name, Stillwater.

The sun had set before we finally arrived at Sioux Charlie Lake. I sprawled out on my back in the still-damp grass, and my dog flopped down beside me. After a few minutes I got up and said, "Come on, O'kohome, we've got to go a little farther."

O'kohome looked up at me. Nothing moved but his eyes.

"I guess you're right," I said, as I reached down and scratched behind his ears, then unsnapped the rope from his harness. I shared a little jerky with him, and ate the only apple I had brought. I pulled out my sleeping bag and crawled in.

O'kohome's growl woke me. It was totally dark, and I could hear twigs snap as something came toward me through the brush. I knew my bow and arrows would be useless in the dark, so I reached for my knife. Whatever it was kept coming until I was sure it was only a few yards away. Then it suddenly went crashing away through the timber. Twice more I heard something moving in the forest, but I thought it sounded like something small.

I waited for the sunrise but it never came. Instead, dark storm clouds covered the sky, and a cold wind whistled down the lake. Was this what I was to face for three months? Was winter coming already?

I put my caribou skin sleeping bag on the sled, and tied the canvas tarp over everything to be sure it stayed dry. I walked out into the forest and looked for tracks, or some sign of whatever it was that had disturbed us during the night but found nothing. Was this whole trip going to be a series of unsolved mysteries?

I snapped the rawhide tug rope onto O'kohome's harness, and we began pulling the sled up the trail that paralleled the shore of Sioux Charlie Lake. The lake was not much wider than the river that flowed out of it. The only real difference was that instead of the rapids and falls we had seen yesterday, it was still, quiet water, except for the waves produced by the wind. The widest place I saw was hardly more than a hundred feet. It was much easier pulling the sled on the level ground than up the steep rocky trail we covered yesterday.

A couple of miles up the lakeshore, I left O'kohome with the sled to see that no animals got into our food. I spent the afternoon exploring for the best way up into the valley that Jose and Roger had named Grizzly Valley, when we had come up to locate my campsite.

When I got back, a young couple was sitting on a rock not far from my sled. They were from the Czech Republic and had been watching to see who drove the dog sled. They were surprised to see that I was a teenager, instead of the old-timer they expected. They said they had been backpacking across the wilderness area for more than a week and had been hit by snow on the last pass. They said that we should all be out of the mountains in a day or so—before the snow hit down here, too. When I told them that I was just beginning three months in the wilderness, they could hardly believe it.

Then the girl looked at me and said, "Oh, of course, you're a native, an American Indian. I suppose this is a normal thing for you. We have read a lot about your people. We admire them and their way of life, and their knowledge of nature."

They still had enough freeze dried food for another day or two and would be out tomorrow, so they insisted I join them for dinner and help eat it up. They talked and talked about all the great country they had seen, and about how envious they were of me spending, more time in the Beartooths.

The rain ended just before we crawled into our sleeping bags and the next morning the sun came over the mountains into a blue sky. My Czech friends insisted on staying long enough to give me some help. They left their packs, and the three of us pulled the sled up the steep mountainside. A short way up the mountain, we looked at the cliffs over to our right and saw a cave. They wondered if it might be an "Indian cave." I laughed and told them I doubted that, but we left the sled and climbed to the cave. There was no indication anyone had ever had a fire in it, but I said that, except for the smelly packrat nest in the back, it would be a good shelter from a storm.

These friends were a godsend when we had to lift the loaded sled across fallen logs. Without them I would have had to unload it a half-dozen times. When we finally reached the area where the ground leveled off, where there was open timber and a fairly good elk trail to follow, they turned back, but not before inviting me to come to Europe to backpack in their mountains next summer.

I stopped at the upper end of the beaver pond and watched two beavers dragging pieces of an aspen tree that they had cut up into the water. They were working very ambitiously, and I realized they were trying to get as much food stored for the winter as possible. I wanted to stay to watch them anchor the wood in the bottom of the pond where they could get at it to eat the bark when the pond was frozen over, but the sun had already set and I had to move on.

By the time I reached the big tree where I planned to make my permanent camp, it was almost dark. But not dark enough to keep me from seeing the fresh claw marks on the tree, about as high up as I could reach. That had to be a grizzly, and a very large one!

I walked about a hundred yards up the edge of the lodgepole pine forest and searched till I found a widow-maker, a dead tree that had fallen and was leaning against a live one. I threw my rope over the leaning one about twenty feet from the ground. I made two trips back to the sled to get my food. I tied the two bags onto the rope and pulled them up plenty high so a grizzly couldn't reach them.

The next morning I found fairly fresh bear signs in four places nearby and damp soil below a big hole where a bear had dug out a ground squirrel or a marmot. There was one clear hind foot track about a foot long.

I called, "Come on O'kohome. We're finding us a new home."

We spent the morning climbing west across a high rocky ridge. O'kohome left me and headed down into another wide valley. As I trotted down the slope, I called to him a couple of times but got no answer. I figured he must be on the trail of something. I stopped for a drink at a tumbling mountain stream, then called O'kohome again. He answered with one bark and I saw him on the slope ahead. When I got to him, he was sitting with a freshly killed rabbit between his feet. I scratched him behind the ears and said, "Got our lunch ready for us, have you?" I looked around and added, "You know something? I think you found a perfect campsite. Maybe I'll put the tipi right where you're sitting."

On the north and south sides of the campsite, the rocky sides of the ridge dropped away sharply, but the grassy east end ran gradually down about a hundred yards to the brook I had just crossed. Tall trees on the north slope of the ridge and a high rocky bluff on the west would protect us from the cold north and west winds of winter. The open view to the east and south would let in the warmth of the early morning sun and provided a magnificent view of rugged snowcapped mountain peaks. About a hundred yards up the ridge, just below the high cliffs, I found a tree with a large limb from which I could hang my food to keep it out of the reach of grizzly bears. Although my search of the area revealed no evidence of bears, I knew I would have to be careful not to leave any food out to attract them.

The route I had taken over the rocky ridge from my first campsite would be impossible for the sled, but on my way back I searched up and down the ridge and found two ledges that appeared to lead across it. I checked them out. The lowest and apparently widest ended suddenly in a high cliff. The higher one, although it narrowed to three or four feet in spots, led all the way across.

I camped in the original spot again. Before I left the next morning, I carefully drew a map of the route to the new campsite. I wanted to be sure Roger and Jose could find me if they did get a weekend off and came up to visit.

I put the map in a little zip lock bag, and put it under the flat rock on top of the big one. I loaded our food into the sled and tied everything down. Then O'kohome and I spent the day dragging it over the ridge to my new campsite.

I used one more day getting my camp established and gathering a good-sized pile of wood. I would try to bring in more each day to be sure I had a good supply when cold weather came. Up here, winter could arrive any time.

In a thick stand of lodgepole pine it was easy to find eleven thin, straight trees for my tipi poles. For my small ten foot tipi they only needed to be twelve or thirteen feet long. I dragged them to the spot I had chosen, where I could clearly see the rising sun. There I tied three together into a tripod, and set two more in each of the spaces between them. I tied the cover to the last one before I set it in place, then pulled it around and laced it down the front so that the tipi faced the morning sun, and the back would face the winter winds. Then I slid the tips of the other two poles into the smoke flaps. With them I could move the smoke flaps to draw out the smoke from my fire regardless of the direction of the wind, or cover the opening when it was raining or snowing. I attached the liner to each of the poles inside. Then I dug the sod out of a spot in the center for my fire. I would do my cooking outside for a while, but it would soon be cold enough to need the heat of the fire inside.

I laid my caribou sleeping robes along the inside wall on the right side, my bucket and skillet and my few clothes on the left. When cold days came and I had plenty of time, I would gather some willows and make a good Cheyenne backrest to put at the back, where I would be facing the open door when I was cooking or relaxing.

I stepped outside, backed away and admired the beauty of the white tipi against the deep green of the forest. I was glad that I hadn't let Roger talk me into borrowing his friend's modern backpacking tent. It wouldn't have been nearly as comfortable or roomy, and I couldn't have built a fire inside to cook and keep warm. The double layer walls of my tipi with three inches of air between would give me plenty of insulation, and the angle of the slanted walls was just right to reflect the radiant heat from the fire back down to keep me warm.

O'kohome had been gone since noon, and when he came back he was carrying a snowshoe hare. There were some small spots of white on its dark fur and I realized it was already starting to turn white for the winter that would be here soon. I gave O'kohome a hug and built a hot fire to cook the meat.

By the time we finished eating, the sky was black, lit by a thousand brilliant stars. I took my caribou sleeping bag outside where I could see the whole sky. I lay there on my back and looked up and recalled the legends my grandparents had told me about the different constellations.

When I opened my eyes again, the moon had come up and a few white fleecy clouds were moving across it. In the moonlight the white snow banks on the tops of the mountains at the head of the valley contrasted sharply with the dark, jagged cliffs below them.

It was then that it hit me that I was *really alone*. It could be three months before I saw another human. What was it going to be like not seeing *anyone*? During all my preparation I had shared my thoughts, my plans, my questions. Sharing was the Cheyenne way. I wouldn't be up here today if people hadn't shared with me. I had made some of what I brought, but even that was only because people had shared their skills and know-how, and I had felt secure because they shared their confidence.

I remembered how lonely I had felt when we first moved to Billings from the reservation—even with my family there, and lots of people around. Three months with strangers had been a long time. What would three months alone, really alone, be like? Could I adjust? I would have to. I would force myself. But what if I couldn't find enough food? What if I fell and broke a leg? What if I got sick? You can't pick up the phone and call 911 in the wilderness. I had never really understood before what it would be like to be alone—totally alone!

7

The Hunt

Even though most of my efforts for the first month would have to go into hunting and locating food, I was glad I had not brought a lot of store-bought prepared foods. I enjoyed knowing I was doing everything the old way. With corn meal, jerky, pemmican, and dried fruits and vegetables, I should have nearly enough food to last for a month, if I didn't have to share too much of it with O'kohome. I was counting on his catching most of his own food, but if he didn't, he would need to eat as much of mine as I did.

I decided I would try to save almost all my food for my last month when other food would be very hard to get, except for the cornmeal, of which I had three sacks, one for each month. So, my first big effort was to find some meat, although I wasn't too concerned about getting started. I had worked hard locating my campsite, hauling in my supplies, and getting my camp set up. I wanted to have a day or two to relax and enjoy the beautiful scenery, to explore some of the surrounding area, to see what animals and birds were around. I wondered what animal neighbors I might still have after most of the birds had gone south and the squirrels and marmots were in hibernation.

O'kohome and I sat down in the door of my tipi, and I cut the fourth notch in my coup stick. He took off on the trail after something, but I just sat and enjoyed the view. Two chipmunks dashed by less  than three feet from my mukluks, and one of them stopped to look up at me. I took a small handful of cornmeal and scattered it on a big rock. Soon two camp robbers were sharing it with a magpie. They moved to a spot farther away when a crow swooped down. He looked the cornmeal over, but then flew to the top of one of my tipi poles.

I suppose my sitting there daydreaming about my early hunting experience was really a way of stalling. I had been hunting most of my life, but I had never depended on a bow and arrows to supply my food. I had made good scores in the archery class last spring, but was that sufficient skill for getting my meat? Did I have the stalking skills I would need to get close enough to bring down a deer? I recalled that when I was only six or seven years old, Dad showed my friends and me how to make rubber band sling shots, and we hunted with them. We felt like real up-and-coming warriors, but seldom got any game. I shot a bird once, and the other boys congratulated me. I was the great hunter for the day. Dad saw it and smiled, "Getting to be a real hunter are you?" But when Mother saw it, she said, "Wouldn't you rather see it alive and hear it sing?" I had already been thinking that as the bird hung limply in my hand on the way home. After that I never wanted to shoot anything unless it was something we could eat.

When I was in the fourth grade, I made my first bow and arrows, and did a lot of hunting but not much shooting. My first big success was the time I got a squirrel. Grandpa Red Coyote showed me how to skin and dress it. He had made sure that I kept every bit of the meat, and that I also took good care of the skin and stretched it properly so Mother could use it for liners in mittens she made for me that fall. "Don't waste anything," Grandpa said. "If you don't make sure every part of what you get is used, you can't expect more game to come to you." I knew Grandpa was serious about that, but Dad never emphasized those things. I always had a feeling that, inside, he laughed at Grandpa's being so insistent on following the old ways, and didn't take the old Indian spiritual ideas very seriously.

Anyway, two friends and I built a fire and roasted the squirrel. I don't suppose it was cooked very well, but I could still remember how good that squirrel tasted just knowing I had gotten it myself.

We moved to town for the year that I was in the fifth grade, and the only time I ever hunted with my bow again was the day that Grandpa died, when I went out and actually killed a wild turkey for the feast after the funeral.

I got my first rifle on my twelfth birthday, when we were back on the reservation. It was a little single shot .22, and I began to bring home a rabbit once in a while for Mother to cook for dinner.

Grandfather Wolf Runner took me on my first deer hunt when I was fourteen. On that hunt he taught me a lot about finding deer and stalking them. But, of course, we were hunting with Grandpa's rifle, an old 300 Savage. I wished now that we had hunted with a bow and arrows. I would feel a lot more confident.

The first deer I saw when I hunted with Grandfather was a big buck with huge antlers. I didn't consider shooting it because Grandfather had told me their meat was tough and strong, especially in the fall. That buck would be all right for the "great white hunters" who came out West, looking for trophy antlers to take home to prove their prowess. We were after meat for the winter. The second was a large one, without antlers. I had raised my rifle to shoot, but Grandfather quickly said "No!" I lowered the rifle and he said, "Look closely." A moment later, a fawn stepped out of the brush, and Grandfather said, "Be careful that you never shoot a doe with a fawn. If you do, you may be killing two deer instead of one, and some future deer besides." I had finally gotten a big dry doe. After I had shot the deer, Grandfather had run to it, but instead of starting to dress it out immediately, he sat down and stroked it tenderly. He took off his beaded bolo tie and draped it across the mule deer's big ears. He closed his eyes and began talking softly, thanking the Creator for leading it to us, and the spirit of the deer for sacrificing herself so that we might eat. He looked up at me and handed me his knife. "You can dress it out now, but be sure you show your appreciation by not wasting a particle of it. Whenever you catch a deer, honor its spirit, and thank the Great Father for it. If you don't, and you never again find a deer when you need one, blame only yourself! Do you expect your human friends to repeat favors for you if you don't show your appreciation?"

The next day Grandfather had gone with me to take a big piece of deer loin to the president of the tribal council, and to several other tribal leaders. After we shared some with several of my friends and their families, there was only a part of one hindquarter left for us. "That's as it should be," Grandfather told me. "Some say a man should share all of his first deer or elk, but we don't usually do this now. In the old buffalo days, sharing was essential for survival. The Cheyenne were all fat or they were all thin."

My reverie was interrupted when a marmot whistled, telling me something was coming. Then I saw O'kohome, trotting back, carrying a rabbit.

"All right, O'kohome, you've done your job. I guess it's time for me to start hunting, too." I checked my quiver to make sure I had several arrows with the razor sharp hunting tips, and several of the blunt-tipped bird arrows. I added my "spirit arrow," then I set out.

O'kohome caught another snowshoe hare that day, and I finally found a grouse. It was the kind we call fool's hen, so it was not hard to get close enough for an easy shot.

That night I got out my fine copper wire and set five snares for rabbits. The next morning I had a cottontail and a whitetail jackrabbit.

I hunted hard for the next few days. I saw a weasel in the meadow, and two mink dodging through a rock slide. I even saw a marten on a tree limb and got a glimpse of a mountain lion. That was a big event for me, actually seeing a cougar in the wild.

In addition to bringing in two more grouse and three more hares, I found two places where wild onions grew, and I dug a few wild carrots, what the Crows called bear root, and what I'd heard others call biscuit root. Their bunches of white flowers were about gone, but the little twigs that held them would stay on. With the help of their fern-like leaves, I would still be able to identify them. I would dig more of both before snow flew and they would keep well in the chilly fall weather. I located a few spring beauty plants and dug the roots. They tasted a lot like potatoes, only with a somewhat nutty flavor. I knew there were lots of them around, but with the flowers long gone, they were difficult to identify. I found some limber pine and was able to get a few nuts, but the squirrels had already taken most of them. I filled my big canvas bucket with wild raspberries, chokecherries, and huckleberries. O'kohome and I ate well and I had a lot of meat and berries drying and smoking in a little shelter I made and covered over with one of my caribou hides to keep the smoke in. I stayed near my camp the next two days to keep the fire going in my smoker, but still was able to get a squirrel and two quail. I gathered a few serviceberries and I filled up on wild raspberries. I located a little pond with water lilies, but I didn't pick any of them yet. They weren't too far away, and although they wouldn't be as tasty as the fireweed and wild onions that I gathered, their roots, leaves, and flowers would continue to provide a little variety in fresh vegetables until the water froze over.

I went down to the little stream below my camp and fished for about three hours before catching one cutthroat trout about eight inches long. I had been told there were plenty of big trout in the Stillwater River, and I would have no trouble catching all I wanted to eat and dry. Maybe this branch was too small, or maybe this was just a bad day. I convinced myself it couldn't be my lack of skill as a fly fisherman. Anyway, I learned that I wasn't going to be able to rely on fish as my main source of food.

We were eating well, and I was getting some food put away, but not as much as I was going to need. I had counted on deer or other big game. I had seen three elk at a distance in Grizzly Valley, and I had seen one mule deer, but it was far away and running in great leaps. I was going to have to go slowly and quietly, keeping my eyes open, and I would need some of my tracking skills.

For the next two days, I hunted deer from sunrise until dark. I left my dog in camp so he wouldn't scare the deer, and he could keep other animals from getting into my smoker and eating my meat and berries. There were many deer and elk tracks but they all appeared to be old ones. I located one whitetail buck with two does and spent a couple of hours trying to get close to them. Finally they saw me and were gone. I tracked them for a while, but lost their trail in the dry rocky soil. One big mule deer buck ran out of the timber, saw me, and stopped. He looked at me for ten or fifteen seconds and was gone  over a high ridge. I knew that I could have gotten him easily with a rifle. I was so frustrated by then that I let fly one arrow, even though I knew he was out of bow and arrow range. I searched but I never did find the arrow. I lost two more trying to get a spruce grouse. I had brought about forty arrows, but I couldn't afford to go on losing them.

I headed back and was not more than a half mile from camp when I saw a bear. It was a black bear, a young one, maybe a two-year-old. I watched him long enough to be sure he was alone. I knew that shooting a bear with a bow and arrows could be dangerous because a wounded bear, even a black bear, was likely to attack. And it would be unlikely that I could kill it with one arrow. But a bear would give both O'kohome and me enough meat for the whole fall. I was feeling desperate. I got out two arrows, held one in my hand with the bow so it was ready for a second shot, and nocked the other, ready to shoot. I had practiced firing two arrows in quick succession. I followed the bear at a distance until he stopped to eat berries from a raspberry bush. He either didn't see me or ignored me as I slipped up to within arrow range. I had a side view, and I aimed at his lower chest. One shot through the heart should kill him. I raised up and aimed carefully, then released the arrow. I had misjudged the distance and it struck several inches higher than I intended. It must have struck his shoulder bone because it hardly penetrated and the arrow fell out as soon as he started to run. He tore through the timber and I pursued him.

He hadn't run more than a hundred yards when he came to a leaning dead tree. As he ran up the slanted trunk, I fired again. This time I hit

him in the hip. He leaped forward and clambered up the tree until he was about twenty feet from the ground, where the trunk was only about four inches thick. The tree swayed and I thought it might fall, but it didn't. The bear reached around and crushed the arrow in his teeth as he pulled it out of his hip. It had hit bone again so had only gone in the depth of the arrowhead. I circled under the tree while the bear looked down at me. I thought, if I shot into his chest from directly below him, I would get him in the heart for sure. I fired. The arrow went into the tree trunk directly between me and his chest and stayed there. I looked the situation over. I had plenty of time. The bear wasn't going anywhere. I backed up to where I could aim directly at his chest without the tree trunk in the way and let fly another arrow. It struck a twig of a tree limb and was deflected enough so it missed the bear completely and went sailing off through the timber.

I pulled another from my quiver, but it was one of those blunt-headed bird arrows. I pulled them all out. All I had left were bird arrows, they were useless. I went in search of the one that had missed. I searched and searched but couldn't find it. I went back to the tree. The bear was still in the same spot, but sitting down on the limb now. I reasoned that if I got right under him, one of those bird arrows might penetrate his hide, and go right into his heart. I got one out, nocked it, pulled it all the way, and let fly. The arrow struck in the exact spot I had intended, but it didn't penetrate his tough hide at all. It just bounced off. But it must have hurt enough to make him angry. The bear gave a combination of a yelp and an angry roar as he spun around and ran two-thirds of the way back to the ground, staring at me angrily. I knew better than to run from a bear—that is a certain way of getting pursued. I backed slowly away, as the bear turned and climbed back up the tree.

As soon as I was out of sight I dashed all the way back to camp. I refilled my quiver with good hunting arrows, took O'kohome, and ran back to the bear's tree. When we got there the bear was gone. I put the dog on his trail, and we tracked him. At one spot he had stopped to dig at a ground squirrel hole. Later he stopped to eat some raspberries. He couldn't be very seriously wounded. But we went on tracking him until dusk. Then we turned back in time to get to camp before it was too dark to see our way.

I had made my caribou hide sleeping bag so that it was a good backpack by itself. I could lay whatever else I wanted to carry in the center of it, and fold the two sides over to the middle, then the lower third up over the center and the top third down. I had thongs to tie it in that position, and two pack straps attached. I put a little of my pemmican and jerky and some dried apples in it, folded it up, and told O'kohome, "We're not coming back until we have a deer." I hung all the meat and berries I had been drying in the tree with the rest of my food to be sure no animals got into it.

We climbed over the rocky ridge back to Grizzly Valley. I checked the rock where I had told Jose I would leave the note. The note and map I had drawn were still there. He and Roger must not have gotten a weekend off because they hadn't showed up. It seemed as if it had been forever since I left them.

We combed that valley from one end to the other all day, but only found a few old tracks, not one deer. Maybe the bears had scared them off.

By noon the next day it was drizzling rain and very cold. I really wanted to go back to my tipi, but I was determined to get our meat. I headed back down toward the Stillwater River and Sioux Charlie Lake. As we climbed over the downed timber between the bluffs, I remembered the cave that the couple from the Czech Republic had thought might be an Indian cave. We climbed over to it. I took a tree limb and used it as a broom to sweep out all the dung, tree limbs, and pine cones stored away by the packrats. With the pine cones and some additional wood I had plenty of fuel to build a fire in the entrance and have a nice warm, dry place to sleep.

When we awoke the next morning there were about three inches of fresh snow on the ground. We hadn't gone far down the mountain before we came to a spot where five deer had bedded down for the night. The ground where they had lain was still warm. They couldn't have been gone more than a few minutes. The snow made it easy to track them and to walk silently. I told O'kohome to stay behind me as

I tracked the deer down the hill. I could see the broken twigs where they had browsed as they walked.

When I finally got my first glimpse of the deer, they were grazing at the edge of a wide meadow. The narrow Sioux Charlie Lake ran along the other side of the meadow less than a quarter of a mile away. I slipped silently down to the edge of the timber and crouched behind the bunch of brush nearest to them. They were almost too far for an arrow to have any killing power even if it could reach them. But there was no chance of getting any closer without being seen. I took a good hunting arrow, pulled it to the hilt, and let fly. It dropped and stuck into the ground about fifteen feet short of the closest deer. The young buck raised its head, looked around, and started walking the other way. I shot again, higher this time, but by now, the deer was farther away and the arrow again fell a few feet short.

Other deer looked up this time, but they didn't know what had disturbed them and they went back to grazing, walking slowly away from me. I slipped back into the timber and circled around the end of the meadow. There was a bank above the lakeshore, just high enough so that, by crouching as I walked, I could keep out of sight. O'kohome seemed to understand what I was doing and crept silently a few feet behind me. Several times I raised up just enough to see over the bank and watch the deer to see which way they were headed, then I moved in that direction.

Finally they seemed to be headed toward a narrow, shallow part of the lake where it would be easy for them to cross. I crouched there, behind the bank, bow in hand, waiting. It must have been fifteen minutes more before they finally got to a spot very near to me and raised their heads and started walking toward me and the lake. They were going to cross just to my left. The one that was nearest to me was a young spike-horn

buck. Just what I wanted! I waited until it was less than twenty feet from me before I raised up and released my arrow. All the deer leaped and ran past. My arrow found its mark exactly where I wanted it to, in the middle of the young buck's chest. The deer staggered but kept on running. A few feet past me it would be in the lake, and I'd be lucky if I ever got it out. Maybe it was all the practice I had had for football, but I didn't stop to think. As it ran by, I dropped my bow and made a rush and a flying tackle. My shoulder hit the deer as my arms went around its neck. It sprawled on the ground with me on top of it. I held its antlers to the ground as I slid around and straddled it to keep out of the way of its flailing hooves. Then I pulled out my hunting knife to cut its throat. O'kohome had his teeth in its nose helping to hold it down.

I didn't even think of Grandpa's ceremony of thanking Mother Earth and the spirit of the deer until I had nearly finished dressing it out. I sort of laughed as I thought of how sure Grandfather would be that no other animals would offer themselves to me. At least I would follow the old Cheyenne policy of using every particle of the deer that could possibly be used.

Even though the snow made it easier to drag, by the time I got it dressed out and we had pulled it up the mountainside as far as the cave, I realized that we couldn't get it much farther that day. The next morning I walked to the tipi and got the dog sled. Back at the cave, I loaded the deer onto it and O'kohome helped me pull it back to camp.

GRANITE PEAK FROM THE TOP OF FROZE-TO-DEATH PLATEAU

8

The Climb

By the next day the snow was all gone, and the weather was almost like summer. The tops of the two mountains at the head of the valley were still covered, and there was a more distant snow-covered peak that showed up between them. It was a very high rugged peak. Since I was a tiny child, my friends and I had always enjoyed climbing the rocky cliffs above our home in Lame Deer. So whenever I see cliffs and rocky mountains, I start studying them to figure out what route I can take to get to the top. Of course the hills on the reservation don't compare with these high-jawed, craggy mountains. Regardless of what I had told Tobie about liking to climb, I had never climbed a real mountain. But I thought I could see a route that just might get me to the top of this one.

I wondered what mountain it was and how high. I got out my forest service map of the Beartooth Wilderness Area and studied it. That must be Granite Peak. It had to be! The highest peak in Montana! Imagine the view from the top of that! But, of course, I knew that it would be absolutely foolish to think of climbing it alone. I'd have to put those thoughts out of my mind.

I wanted to climb some nearby mountain. Tobie and I had discussed it. If I was going to do it, I would have to do it soon. But I put it out of my mind as I went to work finishing my preparations for the winter. I spent a couple of days cutting up and drying the deer meat. I also gathered some wild onions and other herbs and dried them to go with it. Then I spent most of my time for three days gathering and stacking firewood. I would need a big stack when the weather turned cold.

But I also took time to enjoy the animals and the scenery. I hadn't realized how spectacularly beautiful this valley was. Now that I knew we had plenty of meat, and I could think of the animals as my friends instead of food, it seemed there was always some animal in sight. In the evening, I sat by the fire roasting a piece of venison and eating fresh berries I had picked that afternoon, and gazed up at the brilliant stars in an unbelievably clear dark sky. Then I got into my warm caribou robes and drifted to sleep as the fall temperature dipped to below freezing.

Chipmunks and camp robbers greeted me when I got up. Later in the day, three deer strolled through my camp, stopping to look around before going on. One of them stayed and was in sight the rest of the morning.

That evening O'kohome and I were sitting in the door of the tipi watching the birds and enjoying their songs when a skunk came out of the forest and trotted by not six feet in front of me. O'kohome started to jump out at her, but I held him down and wished he would stop struggling. I didn't want her to see him moving and become alarmed, and I didn't want to speak to him, since even that might disturb her. Three half-grown youngsters came romping after her. They stopped to sniff the ashes of my campfire, then trotted on.

Several nighthawks darted back and forth above me, their paths as wildly erratic as those of the insects they pursued. One of the nighthawks uttered its series of short nasal calls after each of its short fluttering dashes as it climbed an erratic path hundreds of feet into the air. Then it folded its wings and dived to within a few feet of the ground emitting a booming call as it swooped gracefully, crossing directly in front of me, and zoomed south till it was just a dot above Granite Peak. The last rays of the setting sun had turned the snow patches that capped the peak into blazes of crimson. I wished I could watch that sunset from the top. A foolish thought, especially for someone who had never climbed a real mountain. But hadn't everyone, except Tobie and Jose, doubted my ability to spend three months up here alone? And here I was, doing great, having the time of my life. I remembered what Tobie had told me about Admiral Byrd: "It wasn't experience, or knowledge, or training that enabled him to spend a winter alone in the unexplored Antarctic. It was his desire, his determination, and his belief in himself."

What harm would there be in hiking part way up the mountain—as far as I could go? And why wouldn't that be the top? Right then I made up my mind I would climb Granite Peak, or at least I would climb to the foot of it, and part way up. No! I'd do better than that. I'd go all the way to the top. How I wished that Tobie was here to climb it with me!

Before it was too dark, I made sure all my meat and other foods were hung up high enough so there was no chance of a bear getting to them. I hung a separate little pack of meat and dried fruit so it would be ready to take with me.

As soon as it was light enough to see, I put the little sack of food, my warm parka and gloves together, folded my sleeping bag around them, swung the pack on my back, and said, "Come on, coyote-dog. We're going on the adventure of our lives." O'kohome always seems to interpret my moods and mirror them. That morning he kept running excitedly forward, and looking back to see why it was taking me so long.

I hiked south, up the long valley in which I was living. As I stepped over numerous rivulets, the creek I followed kept getting smaller. In several places, where the creek plunged over high waterfalls, I had to climb high on the mountain side to get around them. Finally I came to the springs that were the source of the creek and took a big drink of water before I climbed on up.

I passed the last few scraggly trees of timberline and kept on climbing. Finally I came to what I assumed was the top of the Beartooth Plateau. "The largest continuous area above timberline in the U.S.," someone had told me, and it was easy to believe it. It wasn't a flat, high tableland as the geography books described a plateau. It was a rough land of rocks and cliffs. Except for the numerous high mountain peaks that rose above it, it looked crossable in any direction. There were many big, permanent-looking patches of snow, but I was glad to see that the new snow from last week's storm had melted off. There was a whole range of high mountains ahead, not just one, but I was certain that the highest one, the peak that I had been able to see from below, was Granite Peak. I started in that direction.

Although there was more rock than soil, the spaces between the rocky ridges and promontories were mostly soil covered with vegetation. There were still a few tiny flowers, among them some Indian paintbrush nestled between the many other miniature plants.

As I walked along enjoying the flowers, I spotted a ptarmigan. I wouldn't have seen it except for the white spots on its back. It was pecking away at some little four-inch-high snow willows. Remembering that watching the ptarmigan was a good way of learning which plants and berries were safe to eat, I picked a few of the willow stems and chewed on the leaves and bark. Suddenly a half dozen more ptarmigan flew up from almost between my feet; I hadn't even seen them. They landed on a rock slide not far away so I climbed up there and sat down. Except for the one with white on it, I couldn't locate any of them till one hopped up on the top of a rock and chirped. Its color was the same as the rock so it looked almost like another rock balanced there. I knew that in a couple of weeks they would all be pure white, except their black eyes, but they wouldn't be any easier to spot because all this high country would be covered with snow.

As I stood up to move on, I heard a high-pitched squeak. I stopped and stood perfectly still until there was another squeak. Then I located the cony, a tiny creature, rabbit-like except that his ears were small and round, and he had no tail. He was perched on the tip of a rock, and he, too, looked so much like the rock it was no wonder that I couldn't locate him until his squeak told me where to look. O'kohome and I sat down and watched as he ran out along the hillside and gathered blades of grass and brought them back to spread out on a rock to dry. He worked so hard and fast to gather a lot of hay, it was obvious he anticipated a long cold winter. I said to O'kohome, "Maybe I'd better check our food supply to see if we've put enough away."

I stopped frequently to enjoy the ever-changing views of the high rocky ridges, the tumbling streams, the lakes, and the flowers. As I came over a ridge and looked down at two small lakes, two elk were grazing along the shore of the nearest one. They ignored me as I walked along the opposite shore.

In the creek that led from one of the small lakes to the other was a small waterfall. As I passed it, I saw a cutthroat trout jump the fall and stopped to watch as another, then another tried to jump it but fell back. The main waterfall was only about four feet high and three feet wide, but there were more small ones above it. Only about a fourth of the trout that jumped made it successfully over the falls. I wondered how many attempts some of them made before they finally reached the stream above. How many attempts would it take me to reach the top of Granite peak? I doubted that I would be as persistent as those trout were.

Several of the trout missed the stream above and hit the rocks beside the falls. They fell back down, landed on the rocks beside the stream then flopped several times before they finally fell into the stream, where they could try again. O'kohome stood on a rock above and watched excitedly. I climbed down to the bottom of the falls. When the next trout tumbled back onto the rocks at the bottom, I caught it in both hands then climbed up to the stream above. O'kohome stood beside me and wagged his tail as I released the fish into the stream.

I walked on purposefully, but also paused frequently, not so much to rest as to enjoy each new view as I came around a ridge. I was here to enjoy the country, not to punish myself. My goal was to climb the mountain, but if I paused to watch a deer with a fawn, the mountain would still be there.

I came over a ridge and looked down into a deep gorge. It must have been more than a thousand feet straight down to a long, narrow lake at the bottom. I listened to the roar of three waterfalls that tumbled from the brink of the canyon on the other side, and down into the lake. What was that roar saying to me? To turn back? If Tobie were only here, she would have an interpretation for me, but I was sure it wouldn't be that one!

There was no way I could get to the bottom of that gorge and back up the other side, but maybe if I followed it upstream to the west, it would shallow out and I could get around it. A game trail led me west along the canyon rim, but I had to make two long side trips to skirt around two smaller side canyons. I assumed the game trail would eventually lead into the canyon where deer and elk could find water.

Black clouds moved over the top of the ridge above me. The wind switched direction and blew drops of icy cold rain in my face. Several bolts of lightning struck the crags above me, but the thunderstorm swept along the top of the ridge and was gone in less than ten minutes.

O'kohome didn't trot along beside me as most dogs would do. I had watched coyotes hunting. They didn't often stay together in pairs. They spread out, following a parallel course, close enough to help each other if they found big game; otherwise each hunted on its own. O'kohome seemed to adopt the system of his ancestors. I had never taken him along when Grandfather Wolf Runner and I hunted because the dog looked so much like his coyote father that any hunter seeing him would be likely to shoot him. Today, he stayed near me for a while, but as the day wore on he ranged farther off to the side, probably intent on finding us some supper. I never worried about his finding me again. If I turned off the trail he could track me easily.

A couple of miles west, the river that ran through the canyon tumbled over a very high waterfall and above that was another lake. Here the canyon was not quite so deep.

Farther up, beyond another lake, the canyon turned south. I discovered I wouldn't have to cross the canyon at all, only a smaller valley that ran west.

There were moose tracks on the trail, fresh tracks since the shower. I was studying them as I rounded the end of a ridge.

I looked up. There, not a hundred feet in front of me was a big grizzly bear. He stopped, stood up on his hind feet, and looked at me. He dropped to all fours, took a few slow steps forward, and made a low growl, chomping his teeth together and swinging his massive head.

My instinct was to run, but all the things I had been taught flashed through my mind. Never, never run from a bear: that ensures pursuit. Don't look him in the eye: that is a challenge.

I looked off to the left side of him, then very slowly backed off, moving down the bank on the left side of the trail. The grizzly stopped, and turned his head a little to the right. Slowly he backed up a couple of steps, then turned and climbed up the bank on the right. As I continued to slowly back down the hill, the grizzly proceeded across the ridge above me.

I climbed back to the trail. Now I could see occasional claw marks in addition to the moose tracks.

The game trail turned and led down into the upper end of the valley. I followed it as it would get me down into a few timberline trees where I could find wood for a fire. I walked slowly around the point of another ridge, watching carefully. A big bull moose was grazing slowly down the other side of a small ravine. I moved down my side of the ravine, not approaching him directly but gradually getting closer. He ignored me. By the time we got into the first timberline trees I was not a hundred feet from him. I wished I had a camera. I sat down and watched him go down into the heavier timber.

There was a small stream tumbling down the bottom of the ravine. I took a big drink, then sat down and studied the mountain that was straight south at the head of the valley; it was like a wall of rock. I was sure the north side would be impossible for anyone to climb. It didn't look like the west side was much better. Maybe, just maybe, if I went around to the east side it would be better. It didn't look quite as steep. O'kohome came trotting up from behind me with a big marmot dangling from his jaws. How he had managed to sneak up on it, I don't know. I took time to gather a little wood and cook the marmot. It made a much better lunch than the jerky I had brought, and it looked like I would be needing the jerky before I got to the top of that mountain.

I started on and came over a little rise. There in front of me was a lake that ran clear to the base of the mountain. I guessed that it must be more than a half mile long. The west shore would be easier to follow, but there would be no way to get past the cliffs that dropped straight into the lake. I started up the east shore. It was nothing but a boulder field of huge jumbled rocks. Some of the time, I could jump from one to another. Other times, I had to climb up and over the big ones. Several times, I had to give O'kohome a boost to the top of one; he was getting more worn out than I was.

By the time I reached the saddle between Granite Peak and the mountain east of it that my forest service map identified as Froze-to-Death Plateau, the sun had set, and the temperature was dropping. I searched for a spot where I could sleep, but there was no place, nothing but jumbled rock. If I was going to climb the mountain the next day, I would have to have a drink, and there was obviously no water on the side of that mountain.

I turned and studied Froze-to-Death Plateau. The top was not too far above me, and I could see several patches of snow and wet rocks below them.

By the time I reached the top it was nearly dark, but I could still see well enough to find a little patch of level ground to sleep on. Only a few yards away a little stream of clear water trickled from under a big snow bank.

A brisk breeze had come up, or maybe there was always one on the plateau! There was nothing that I could get behind for shelter from the

FLINTS ROUTE UP GRANITE PEAK

A. The beginning of the climb from the "saddle" between Granite Peak and
    Froze-to-Death Plateau.
B. Top of the snowfield where Flint crossed.
C. The "chimney" through the cliffs, where Flint left his dog, O'kohome.
D. The spot where he met the other climbers.
E. The "notch" where he left his companions.
F. The six-inch ledge which took him across to another "chimney".
G. The rock that formed a bridge and a keyhole through the ridge.

icy wind. It was easy to see why it was called Froze-to-Death Plateau. Even though I had my caribou skin sleeping bag and the warmth of my dog as he cuddled up against my back, I was not comfortably warm as I went to sleep.

About the middle of the night, O'kohome wiggled around enough to wake me. In the light from a quarter moon, I could see three mountain goats pawing the ground about fifteen feet from me, where I had urinated before I crawled in.

"You won't find much salt there," I said aloud. They ignored me and wandered around my camp for about fifteen minutes before they moved on.

I woke up to the light of the sun rising over the mountain range in a blaze of glory. I wished Jose and Roger could be here to enjoy it with me. Or Tobie!

I studied the mountain carefully, trying to find a possible route to the top, then I climbed down to the saddle between the mountains. By the time we got there, a slow drizzling rain had started. I looked at O'kohome, shivered, and said. "It's probably a lot colder up on the mountain, O'ko. Do you think we ought to try and go on?"

O'kohome wagged his tail, pranced around me, and started up the slope. The rain didn't dampen his spirits at all. I knew I wouldn't want to try to negotiate those cliffs with a big pack on my back so I rolled up my caribou sleeping bag and stuffed it as far as I could under a big boulder. I only took my parka and my survival kit.

The first part was hard climbing but it didn't present any real difficulties. There was a long snow bank on our left. It should have been a smooth route, but, after a summer of melting and freezing, the top layer was mostly ice, and I couldn't stand up on it. I kept climbing up the rocks, occasionally having to lift O'kohome up over a small cliff. After about an hour, I came to a spot where the mountain rose straight up ahead of me, seemingly forever. On my right was the perpendicular north side of the mountain, and on my left the top of the snow bank. I edged my way along the top of that snow bank, trying to kick footholds in the icy snow, and clinging to any handholds I could find in the rocks above. O'kohome tried to follow in my footsteps. Twice he slipped, but managed to scramble back to the top.

Beyond the snowfield was a long series of cliffs. I started climbing up and down along the mountainside below them looking for a way up. I located a couple of crevices that I thought might be possibilities, but I could see that they dead-ended about half way up. I began to doubt there was a way past them.

A nighthawk dived from above, making his booming sound as he zoomed just below my feet, then he began his erratic climb, dodging back and forth along the cliff above, even darting into a fissure half way up. That wasn't just a cranny. It was a *chimney*, a crevice between two rocks that went all the way to the top. I climbed up to it. It varied in width from two to four feet. It was a lot taller, but not too different from the one I had scaled many times to get to the top of the ridge above my home in Lame Deer. Back home, O'kohome always took a long way around and met me at the top. There wasn't another route here. If there was, I'd be taking it.

"O'kohome," I said, "there's no way I can take you on up from here. You're just going to have to wait here for me. Stay!"

I put my feet against one side of the crevice and my back against the other and inched my way up. My dog stood at the bottom and whined, but I ignored him.

It was much higher on the mountain, and more than an hour later, when I edged around some rocks looking for a way past a particularly steep spot. As I came around the ridge, I could see the mountainside ahead. Below me, and quite a distance to the right, I spotted three climbers. After watching them for a few minutes, I realized that they had a rope between them. I reasoned that they must be experienced mountain climbers, and they probably could pick a better route than I could. I kept climbing up, but edged my way over toward their route when I could.

When I was nearly above them, I stopped and waited. They saw me and waved, then angled up to where I was sitting. They stopped to talk. The two men and one woman were from Maine. They had started two years ago spending their summers trying to climb to the highest spot in every one of the fifty states.

"This is our forty-ninth," The woman told me. "We left it for close to the end because it is technically the hardest. The only one we will have left after we climb this one will be Mount McKinley in Alaska."

I asked if they had had some other pretty tough climbs.

"Sure have, especially Kansas," one of the men said.

"Kansas?"

They all laughed, then the woman explained, "Had to walk to the middle of some guy's cow pasture." She looked around. "Where are your companions? Is that who you're waiting for?"

"No. I'm climbing the mountain alone."

"Alone! Really? We wouldn't even attempt it without at least the three of us, or without ropes. Oh, you're an American Indian, aren't you? And you're from Montana. Well, of course! I suppose this is old stuff to you."

I switched the topic by saying, "Well, at least it will be easier since the rain stopped. I was afraid it might make the rocks too slippery." I didn't want to tell them I had never used ropes. And I definitely wasn't about to tell them I had never been on top of a real mountain. However, I did feel pretty confident about my ability as a rock climber. I had done that all my life right near my home in Lame Deer.

They suggested I take the lead as we climbed on up the ridge. A half hour later we climbed into a big notch in the ridge that separated the east and south sides of the mountain. Above us were only some impossible looking cliffs. I started trying to locate a way up through them. I thought with their ropes and spikes they could maybe negotiate them. I wasn't so sure about myself. They stood discussing that for a minute, then turned their attention to the slope to our left. It was not as steep, but was covered with lots of loose jumbled rock that could roll right out from under you. I didn't like the looks of that either.

When they decided to try that route, I told them, "I'll stay here till you get above all that scree. Don't want to get hit by a rock or roll one down on you."

"That's a good idea. We'll have to be awfully careful of that ourselves. We don't want one of us climbing above another."

I watched as they angled across the mountainside. I was glad to see that one always went on ahead, then another, then the third. Two of them always anchored on something solid; they could do that. Being alone, I wouldn't have that security. Twice small rocks slithered down the slope below them. Then a big boulder rolled from under the feet of the man in the middle. He slid a few feet, far enough to throw the woman behind him off balance. They were both scrambling, flattening themselves out on the rocks to keep from sliding on down the mountain. I jumped to my feet and started to run toward them, then realized I was too far away to help. If I tried to run across that scree, they would likely be the ones trying to do the rescuing.

The boulder loosened a half dozen others that leaped and bounded down the mountain. I could hear rocks rolling and thudding far below. I worried about O'kohome. I thought he was farther to the right, but I couldn't be sure.

As they moved on, I studied the cliffs above and to my right, trying to see a possible route by which I could get to the top. I thought I could see one possibility, but knew it would be risky. About ten minutes later, the three climbers reached a steeper spot and crouched on the loose rocks as they talked together. Then they turned back.

When they got back to me, their leader said, "We're going down. We don't think we can do that cliff above here. And those clouds below us are moving up. We could be in a storm before long."

"I'll probably be close behind you," I said. "But I'll climb over to our right to the foot of those cliffs, and get the view from there. I'd never forgive myself if I turned back before I went as far as I could. Oh, yes. When you see a coyote below those cliffs near the bottom, don't try to kill it. That's my dog, O'kohome."

I found enough footholds and handholds to get to the foot of the cliffs, but couldn't see any kind of crevice up through them. If I tried to continue on across from where I stood, I would be on a narrow ledge that varied from about four or five inches to a foot wide, and below me would be the valley floor several hundred feet straight down. The cliffs above the ledge were almost perpendicular, but slanted enough so I could stand on the ledge if I leaned against them. It looked like a long way to the other end. Well, I would inch along it to the first bend, where I could see what the rest was like. Keeping my toes on the ledge and my tummy against the cliff, I edged along. Most of the way I could find little notches in the face of the cliff where I could hang on with my fingers. I got around the bend and the ledge continued. Finally, after what seemed like hours, I came to a chimney that would take me to the top of the cliffs. When I was at the top of the cliffs, I angled back across the mountain, climbing steadily. At one point I could see back down to where I had left the other climbers. They were still sitting where I left them. I yelled and waved, and they waved back, before I started on up.

I kept angling across to the ridge. I reached it at a spot where a huge rock had fallen across a notch making a bridge between two points. Before I crossed through the passageway under the bridge, I looked down and thought about how much harder it would be to see my footholds going down and realized I would be taking my life in my hands at every step.

As I climbed on up, I turned frequently to enjoy the view, looking over the tops of all those peaks that had been on the skyline earlier.

I wished Tobie could be here to enjoy this final achievement with me. I knew how she enjoyed climbing! Then a blast of icy wind reminded me that I couldn't waste time daydreaming.

Just as I scrambled over the last cliff and could see the top ahead, the storm hit. The wind was so strong that I could hardly stand up. Fortunately, the wind was from my back or I might have had to go back. I was following a very narrow ridge with an almost perpendicular drop-off which fell hundreds of feet down on both sides. As I struggled up the last few hundred feet to a very steep collection of big boulders, to a granite knob at the summit, the blast kept me hanging on. When I turned to look back, icy crystals of snow stung my face. Still, I was elated to be on the top of the highest peak in Montana!

I got down on all fours and crept to where I could see down on the far side. I didn't dare stand up. I could be swept off the top. I looked down into the blackness of the storm. It appeared to go straight down forever. It would be forever if I let myself get torn off of here. I turned, crawled back from the edge, and looked around. I wished I could see the view—something besides blackness and white snow crystals.

I wondered if this snow and rain had also hit the mountain below. If those cliffs I had doubts about were slick with rain, or maybe even ice, how would I get down? There was no wood up here for a fire, not even a flat place to lie down. My warm caribou sleeping bag was waiting for me at the bottom of the mountain!

I turned and started letting myself down over the series of boulders. I hadn't gone more than fifty feet when I saw the three climbers come over the rocks below me. Their leader shouted to me over the blast of the storm. "We couldn't let a lone climber pass us up, so we decided we had to go as far as possible. Followed your route. You got us to the top."

I waited until they were ready to go down, and we climbed down together. When we reached the cliffs that had almost stopped us from getting to the top, they tied a rope around my waist and I backed over the edge and down the side of the cliff, not worrying about footholds. Then I watched as they each rappelled down. I determined that I would learn those techniques some day.

At the lower cliffs, I led them to the chimney which gave them an easier route than they had used on the way up. O'kohome was waiting at the bottom of the cliff. He danced around, overjoyed to see me. I wished he could have gone all the way with me, but realized that being on top wouldn't have meant a thing to him. It was Tobie who should have been with me. I could see her grin, and feel the warmth of the hug she would have given me when we climbed over the rim at the top.

I looked back up at the top of the mountain. The mass of it was overwhelming. I knew that I had measured myself against a mighty big stick and had measured up. It gave me a new feeling about myself. Not a feeling of having conquered the mountain, as much as of having conquered myself, and my hesitancy at tackling what appeared impossible. It was a feeling that I would carry with me for a long time. I'd have to think of a good symbol to carve on my coup stick to commemorate this conquest.

9
The Quest

The night after I got back was cloudless. I remembered the mountain goats that had visited me at the foot of Granite Peak. I looked at the black sky loaded with brilliant stars, and I decided I would sleep outside. There would soon be plenty of nights when I would have to sleep inside my tipi to keep warm. I lay on my back, my left hand on O'kohome who had curled up beside me. The Milky Way was a river of jewels from horizon to horizon. A meteor streaked across the sky. I looked up at the chain of galaxies stretching across the universe and tried to recall all the legends of the stars and their origins that Grandfather Wolf Runner had told me when I was a youngster. I knew that most of the Cheyenne boys my age had never heard many of the old legends. I was glad that I had a grandfather who didn't hesitate to turn the TV off to tell me stories.

I was wakened when O'kohome stood up and growled. I grabbed his harness to hold him until I could see what had alarmed him. The moon had risen and was lighting the camp brightly.

I heard a man's voice; at least it sounded like a man's voice. I listened, but I couldn't distinguish any words. It sounded like the voice of someone trying to talk with their mouth tightly closed. A fainter, apparently younger voice answered. I could see no one.

A large porcupine walked near me on her way to my campfire, where she stopped her talking to gnaw on my frying pan. Two half-grown youngsters came wobbling by and squeezed in beside her. They continued to make talking noises. They must have been trying to get the salt off my skillet. I was glad I had put my axe in the tipi. I had heard that porcupines could eat up the handle of an axe to get the salt from the sweat on the handle.

One of the young ones walked over and sat up on his haunches as he observed the tipi. I was glad I had tied the door shut. If they got inside, I'd have to get up and drive them out. It's hard to tell what they would have destroyed. The mother turned and looked at me and said several more "words" before she walked away, with her "kids " trotting after her. I called, "Goodbye! Come again." O'kohome jerked and pulled, wanting to chase them.

"No, O'kohome. They're friends. Don't hurt them." If I could convince him to leave them alone the next time he saw them, it could save him from being badly injured by their quills.

I laughed, thinking what Tobie would say when I told her about the porcupines coming and talking with me. She would probably ask if I had pinched myself to see if I was dreaming.

Grandfather Running Wolf would say the animals were supposed to talk to me—at least if I was on a vision quest. A vision quest! I had laughed at Grandfather when he first suggested I go on one. I had told him those quests were things of the past. No one believed in them any more. But then I had realized that it could be an important part of my time in the wilderness, and Grandfather had made preparation for it an important part of the sweat lodge ceremony. I had sort of pushed it out of my mind since I had been up here. I guess I just wasn't quite sure I could have a vision. As I had told Grandfather, no one had them any more.

I thought back to the many things Tobie and I had discussed on our last evening together in the library before Christmas. Tobie had mentioned vision quests and I had said I thought the men of nearly all American Indian tribes went on them. She had surprised me when she said people from all parts of the world went on fasts, and many of them were really vision quests. They were part of the lives of the prophets of nearly every major religion. The Hindus and the Taoists think they are essential for developing a spiritual life. She said even Christ went on a fast for forty days and had his own vision that guided his life. She mentioned a man named Paul whose vision had completely changed his life as well as the lives of many others down through the centuries. She even knew about Sweet Medicine, the great Cheyenne leader, whose vision forewarned my own people of many of the problems that were coming. She hadn't mentioned a vision quest the night she gave me my "medicine bag," but I was sure that's what she had in mind. I reached for it. Yes, it still hung from the cord around my neck.

I went to sleep, and I dreamed. I dreamed that the porcupine, Tobie, and Grandfather were all in my tipi with me, carrying on some kind of a ceremony. Grandfather was praying—thanking the Great Father that he had held off the cold weather long enough so I could go on my vision quest.

When I woke up, the sun was just about to rise. The few stratus clouds above the eastern horizon glowed red as if they were on fire. I stood, and as the first rays of the sun appeared over the horizon, I spread out my arms, looked into the sky, and prayed. I prayed that the winter weather would hold off long enough for me to go on my quest, and I asked for the courage, the strength, and the energy to endure nearly two more months alone.

I went to my bag of supplies and dug out the little envelope that Tobie had enclosed in her letter last February. I read, "Save this. Do not open until the day of your vision quest." Was now the time? No. I had waited this long; I would wait a little longer until I was on the mountain top. I put the envelope in my pocket along with four pieces of yarn and a little pouch of cornmeal.

I cooked a big breakfast of rabbit and corn meal mush, and added a few rose hips. As I shared it with O'kohome, I told him, "Eat your fill. Unless you catch your own, it's your last meal for several days."

I picked up two of my caribou hides and my water bottle. I knew that if I followed tradition I could take nothing else with me. No bow and arrows for defense. No food. But I could have water after sunset. I filled my water bottle when I crossed the stream and started climbing the ridge that separated the valley I was in from Grizzly Valley, where I had first planned to camp. I climbed toward the upper end of the ridge and gathered an armful of sage as I climbed. At the top was a bald knob that should give me an inspiring view in all directions.

O'kohome trotted at my side. I knew I was supposed to go alone; I probably shouldn't even have the company of a dog. But there was no way I could make O'kohome stay away from me for four days, if it took that long to have a vision.

It was a silent and exquisite day. The only sounds were the faint trickle of water in the valley below and the song of a meadow lark. Butterflies flittered along the hillside above me. A chipmunk sat up, flicking his tail, and watching as I passed, but he did not run away.

When I reached the top of the ridge, I found that it was just a jumbled pile of rocks—nowhere that I could possibly lie down—but just to the east was a flat grassy spot. I marked off a space about twenty feet across. The big rocks would be my west boundary. There was a big boulder on the east. I carried rocks to mark my north and south boundaries. I put a smaller rock in between each of these to finish marking the boundaries of the circle within which I would stay. This circle would represent the circle of life, and also the circle of the universe. I got out the four pieces of colored yarn. I walked to the boulder on the east and placed the yellow yarn on it and prayed for wisdom. I took the blue one to the rock on the south and prayed for physical, mental, and spiritual growth. When I put the red yarn on the west, I prayed for courage, and with the white yarn on the north, I asked for strength.

I spread the sage I had gathered on the ground so its aroma rose around me, then I laid one of my caribou skins over it to sleep on. I laid it so that my head would be toward the center of the circle—the center of the universe. I placed my jacket and shirt beside it. Long before my ancestors had moved onto the great plains and hunted the buffalo, they had depended upon the caribou for food and clothing. I was glad I had a caribou hide to drape over my shoulders for warmth.

I pulled out the little envelope Tobie has sent that said, "Do not open until you are on your vision quest." I opened it and read:

> Since I last saw you I have been studying all I can find about the vision quests of Native American leaders, and I have a dream that you will one day be one of those trail-blazers. If you do go on a quest for a vision, I hope the vision you seek will not be a vision just for yourself, or only for the Cheyenne people. Seek a vision for all of us, a vision of how racial snobbery can be erased and all people can become brothers and sisters, united by love and understanding.
>
> Black Elk, the great Sioux leader, had a vision in which he saw the sacred hoop of the Sioux, which had been broken, come back together. Then he saw many other hoops of many other people. Then one great hoop encircled all the people and all the animals, all joining together in a sacred circle of harmony. Crazy Horse, too, had a vision in which he saw many people dancing under the sacred tree. He was surprised to see people of all races and all nations joining in the dancing. I believe in their visions. It is my dream that all the people in each of my five cultural groups will one day join hands in one great circle of understanding. And that all those circles will then join together in one great circle, held together by friendship and love.
>
> I believe the world is moving in that direction, and we are even beginning to include the animals. You can't make all the world join the circle. Neither can I. But we can each, wherever we find ourselves, encourage others to join it. And we can hang on tightly to the hands on each side of us, so that our little part of the circle can never be broken. My hand is in yours. Can you feel it?
>
> This is my vision. What will yours be?
> Tobie

I closed my eyes, then clenched my hand in a tight grip. "Yes, Tobie, your hand is in mine."

My first night on the mountain I didn't expect any kind of dream. It was too soon. I enjoyed a sound sleep and woke up refreshed.

I remembered what Grandfather Running Wolf had told me. "It is useless for you to go on a quest unless you are ready to devote your whole mind and soul to it." I was ready. I got out the little pouch of cornmeal I had brought. It was a symbol of the Creator's generosity to our people, of all the wonderful gifts he had given us. I scattered a little to the east, the south, the west, and the north. Then I tossed a little straight into the air to share with God, Ma'heo'o, the Great Father: a little of what he has given us. I scattered the last at my feet, on Mother Earth, from whence all our food, all the necessities of life have come.

I turned to O'kohome and said, "I'm not leaving here, till I have a vision, so don't go begging me. Now go on and find yourself some dinner. I need to be alone. Go on. Scoot!"

O'kohome left and I sat alone, enjoying the view, trying to concentrate, but on what? I tried to keep my mind concentrated on the spirit, I prayed for purity and the strength to keep my life centered on helping my people, and on Tobie's dream. But my mind wandered. I watched a chipmunk darting around gathering seeds, then running away to hide them so he could come back for more. A big marmot came from his hole under the rocks and looked at me. He whistled his warning, telling all the animals that I was there.

A great bald eagle circled above me. Would that be my totem? I was supposed to have a vision of my future, and to be visited by an animal or bird that would be my guide, my spirit helper. But I was also supposed to have faith that it would happen. Did anyone ever have a vision and a visitation if they didn't have the faith that it would happen? I had heard that some boys had to go on two or three vision quests before they had a vision. Occasionally a young man never had one. He felt disgraced for life. Well, at least if I didn't have a vision, I could laugh it off. It wouldn't keep bothering me—or would it?

Long afternoon shadows crept across the valley. Above me swallows darted and dashed after insects.

About sunset O'kohome came back and kept looking at me as if wondering why I didn't go home and fix some dinner. He started off in that direction once, glancing back as if I should follow, but he soon turned and came back. When I lay down, he curled up at my feet and kept them warm.

I got up hungry, but I told myself I could ignore the feeling. I did until noon when the hunger pangs came back much stronger. All afternoon they made it hard to concentrate on better things. The day wasn't just uncomfortable and long, it was boring. How would I manage the inactivity for two more days, if it took that long to have my vision—as if I really believed I would have one!

I lay down the third night convinced that with the hunger, and the hard ground for a bed, if I didn't have a vision, I would at least have a dream. I wasn't sure what the difference between the two was, anyway. But it didn't matter because, although I woke up several times trying to get comfortable, I had a dreamless night.

At dawn, I watched the millions of stars gradually fading from view. Then I stood and faced the Morning Star, symbol of the Cheyenne, still shining brightly in the east, and I asked the Creator to create within me a vision, a vision of how I could serve Him and my people best, and to give me the spiritual power to carry out that vision.

The birds were singing on all sides of me even before the sun rose into a cloudless sky. I watched it rise and knew that this was the most sacred time of the day. I tried to remember and sing the song a Pueblo elder sang each day as the sun came over the horizon. As the first rays of the sun came above the horizon he would sing, "Rise, arise, arise. Wake thee arise, life is calling thee. Wake thee arise, ever watchful be. For the One God, he is calling thee. For the One God, he is watching thee. All arise, arise, arise."

Surprisingly, in spite of the restless night, I got up refreshed, feeling ready for anything. As soon as I started moving around, O'kohome started jumping around me, wanting some action. I knew he was disappointed that I didn't go running with him. I scratched him behind the ears and said, "Don't be impatient, O'kohome. It's going to be a great day."

The two marmots in the rock pile apparently had decided we were both harmless, and they moved about freely for a while. Then they made a mad rush for their den when a bobcat leaped from the far side and perched on the top of the boulders. I instinctively reached for my bow and arrows, but of course they weren't there. After a moment, he turned away from me and moved into the timber. Two bald eagles circled over the valley for a while, then one of them dived for something in the meadow far below.

I sat as silent and motionless as a tree, absorbing it all. Grandfather had said I should listen to the sounds of nature for they were all voices of the Great One. Today I understood. Every noise seemed to have meaning for me: the songs of the birds, the movements of the animals, the clatter of the grasshopper that flew up, even the chirps and buzzes of the insects. I would let them sink deep into my memory so they would still be with me when I would walk down the crowded streets of the city.

I looked up to the Creator and I asked not only that I be given a vision, but that the vision show me how to do more for my people. And I asked that the vision guide me so that I could face the difficulties of life in a way that would set an example for younger children and influence their lives as well as my own.

I listened to the voices of the aspen leaves as they rustled in the breeze, and the messages in the songs of the birds and the buzzing of the insects. I watched for meaning in the way the lizard stopped and tipped his head as he looked up at me, and the manner in which the chipmunk approached me and even put his front feet on my moccasin and looked up into my face before he scurried away.

When I had scattered the cornmeal I had done it as a sacred act, in recognition of the great gifts that the Creator had given our people. Now it was making the chipmunks stay close a little longer. The finches were hopping around on the rocks hunting the grains the chipmunks left. Their song seemed to have a message for me, a message from the spirit about the value of sharing, of being one with all of nature.

In the afternoon, six elk came out of the timber and grazed across the meadow. Before long a grizzly bear entered the meadow moving very slowly toward them. He got fairly close to them before they suddenly turned and sped away. The grizzly sprang into action and dashed after them. I was surprised to see that he could run as fast as the elk did. At the edge of the meadow, they doubled back past him and he spun in pursuit. Before they got into the timber at the other end, they were outdistancing him and he stopped. He turned and walked in my direction, stopped to eat some berries, then ambled off to the north.

Just as the sun was setting, a coyote howled in the timber not far from me. Several of them answered from across the valley. O'kohome sat back, stuck his nose in the air, and sang out his answer. I watched the swallows zip across the sky like winged bullets. Several bats, then a nighthawk joined them. An hour later, the deeper voices of a pair of wolves echoed across the valley. The screech of a mountain lion, like the scream of a woman, sent chills through me.

I sat quietly, listening to an occasional rustling or snapping noise in the forest. I didn't lie down to rest until the moon came over the

distant mountains. I lay there and thought about all that I had seen that day. Could the fact that so many of the large and powerful animals had shown themselves to me have something to do with the fact that I was on a vision quest? I thought Grandfather would say so. More likely it was simply that I had sat quietly, stayed alert, and observed carefully. I should do it more often.

An occasional mosquito buzzed around me. Tonight they didn't annoy me. I could ignore them. They were just another part of the wonderful natural world I had enjoyed all day. Two nighthawks swooped and glided through the air. I wondered how they could see to catch insects by only the light of the stars. I watched the speed of those nighthawks. I knew that within a month they would be using that speed to get all the way to South America. I wondered if Tobie was still in Peru. Maybe she would see those same nighthawks. Several bats swooped back and forth through the air above me. I knew they were catching hundreds of mosquitoes. Nature seemed to be doing everything to cooperate with me.

It was the fourth night; it should be the last night of my vision quest. It was the night I should have my vision. Surely one of those animals that had shown itself to me that day would be my spirit helper. My spirit helper? Was I actually beginning to think that my quest had some influence on those animals? My scientific mind, all my schooling, said this wasn't possible. If I did see anything tonight, it would just be a dream, maybe induced by my hunger and my wishes, but still just a dream.

No! That night I chose to believe that it would be more than a dream. I was positive I would have a real vision. My spirit helper would show himself to me. Which one of the animals I saw would it be? The grizzly bear? The eagle? I would be satisfied with any of them; even the bobcat, although a cougar would give me more power!

Even if it wasn't the kind of vision I hoped for, if I concentrated on the animals as I went to sleep, I was certain to dream about one of them. I concentrated on the strength, the energy, and the spiritual power of the grizzly, then the eagle, then . . .

I woke with a start. What kind of spirit had touched my arm? I opened my eyes. It was O'kohome, apparently wondering why I was still asleep. The sun was already in the sky. I had slept straight through. No dream. No vision. Nothing!

I should have gone back home to my tipi. But I hated to give up. Everything else on this trip had been so successful—my hunt, my mountain climb. Why should this be a failure? But then, why wouldn't it? I had been saying all along that vision quests were something out of the past. They wouldn't work in the modern world. So why should I be so disappointed? But I was. I felt like a failure. Well, I would stay through the day. The day before had been so interesting, so many animals, so much to think about. Perhaps today would be just as good. Did anyone ever have visions in the daytime? Maybe that's when they came.

I remembered what Grandfather had told me, "It may be that you will not have a vision at first, but do not give up. It may be that your heart is not right. You must trust in the One above. You must let your spirit take over. Only then are you ready to accept a vision and whatever message that vision brings. You must, above all, learn humility."

Maybe that was what I lacked, humility. Maybe I was looking for a great vision for the world when what I needed was a small one to fit my own small self.

O'kohome left shortly after I got up, and he was gone all morning. I watched the marmots, the chipmunks, and an occasional small bird. I wondered what my high school friends would say if they saw me sitting here. If they were here, we would have been hiking, climbing, racing, collecting, achieving. They would never understand that doing absolutely nothing can be a soul filling experience, an achievement.

Late in the morning three ravens began circling above me. There must have been something dead or dying nearby. More than once, during my year on the ranch, I had seen a dozen ravens circling above a dead cow. Once, they started long before the cow died. Maybe some animal was down and about to die. Maybe it was me! Perhaps I had stayed in one spot so long they thought I was crippled and about to die. I laughed and shouted at them, "You won't get me. No way!"

About noon, O'kohome came back carrying a big whitetail jackrabbit. He wagged his tail as he laid it at my feet. At last, we were going to have food even if I wouldn't go out and hunt for it. "No, O'kohome. I'm not going to eat until I go back to camp tonight." But I couldn't discourage him from continuing to hunt food for both of us. I pulled out my pocket knife and skinned and cut up the rabbit, but I fed it all to O'kohome.

I got to thinking about the quest I was on. A vision quest was supposed to be more than just seeking a vision: it was a preparation for life. Sure it was a quest for a spirit helper, but the purpose of that spirit helper, and any dreams or messages that went with it, were for the purpose of making life more meaningful, of having a guide for the rest of life. Maybe if it had been a medicine man who had prepared me for the quest, he would have told me that I was to spend the time planning my future. Maybe if I did some real thinking about the future, I wouldn't think of this quest as a failure. It could still give me a vision of my future. It would be worthwhile even without the traditional vision.

I realized I had never given the future the concern that maybe I should have. I had thought that Grandfather's statement, "The way to prepare for tomorrow is to do your best today. Make today good and tomorrow will be good," meant exactly what it said. But maybe Grandfather was saying more than that. Maybe he was saying that if a person had a vision, a goal, then doing your best today would lead toward that goal.

Tobie was as traditional as they come. She honored all the old traditions. But she had a vision. She had a plan. She even had a scholarship to attend Northern Arizona University, although she wasn't yet a high school senior! Maybe when she had told me about the scholarship she thought it would inspire me to plan for the future. Well, I had enrolled in Upward Bound, as she suggested. But I hadn't really planned what I would do after it. The instructors had said we should get applications in to half a dozen colleges. I had only gotten around to filling out one. I knew the top students would be applying for admission to universities in the fall, while I was up here in the wilderness. I should have done it before I left. Had I missed out? I made up my mind I would start applying as soon as I got back. But for what? I thought over all my abilities, my interests, and the possible careers they could lead to. I had always said I wanted to do something to help my people, the Cheyenne. But what? What could I do without a college education? I also knew that I couldn't be a real success in a career unless it was something I could put my heart into and be excited about. I had better have some definite plans before I went home.

I was still thinking about my plans, and my possibilities, when the sun set behind some dark clouds. O'kohome had been gone all afternoon. Maybe that was good because it had left my thinking uninterrupted, but I wondered where he had gone. I would wait a little longer for him to come back, then I would start back to camp in time to be there before dark. I waited. Did I still have time to make it back?

Suddenly a cold wind hit me. I moved over closer to the big rocks to get some shelter from the wind. A few big drops of water pelted me. There was a blinding light and a loud boom as lightning crashed into the rocks a few feet behind me. Another bolt split the nearest tree to my right. Two more struck on my left. I thought I saw a little blaze and smoke coming from one of the trees. I forsook the small territory I had marked off for my quest as I dashed down to see how much fire there was, to see if I should fight it to prevent a forest fire. But how could I do that? I had no tools; nothing but my little water bottle. Then the rain hit in earnest. I was drenched in a moment. The smoke of the fire turned to steam. In the semidarkness, I stumbled back to my spot and huddled under a bush for what protection I could get. Slush began covering the ground as snow mixed with the rain.

Where was O'kohome? Had he forsaken me? Gone back to the tipi? I needed him. We needed each other for warmth. I had been taught all about hypothermia. It often hit at temperatures well above freezing. I knew that in this storm I could die from it. I would have to get back to my tipi and start a fire. I stood up and took a couple of steps into the wind. That was the way toward camp. I stumbled over a rock and almost fell. I couldn't see a thing; it was totally dark. There was no way I could go anywhere. I could walk into tree branches. I could walk off a cliff. The rain still pelted me. Icy crystals burned my face.

As I watched the powerful forces of the storm, I realized how small and weak I really was. One bolt of lightning produced more power than I could expend in a year. And I knew how humble I must become before I could expect any of the forces of nature or of God to take notice of me. Maybe that was the reason I had not had a vision. Perhaps I had been too proud, had expected too much.

I felt my way back under the bush and curled up between my wet caribou hides to try to stay warm. I called O'kohome several times, but there was no answer. I heard the scream of a mountain lion. What was it doing out on a night like this? Would it find my body in the morning? I only asked that my life be spared, that I not die of hypothermia before morning.

I was sitting on the ground under the bush when a bird swooped down past me and back into the sky. What was it? An eagle? Hardly. When it again swooped down and then landed on the rock in front of me, I could clearly see that it was a nighthawk. It sat tipping its head from one side to the other, examining me. Then it spoke. I was so astonished at its speaking that I almost missed what it was saying. "You have climbed the highest mountain in Montana. Now you must climb the highest mountain of education. But let your desire to help your people be your real guide. That is the Cheyenne way. You will find many obstacles, but you can climb over them, just as you climbed the mountain. I can guide you while you are here, but in the canyons of the city you will need your other spiritual helper. Listen to her."

"Who will that . . ." There was no one to hear my question. The nighthawk had leaped from its perch and zoomed off, up the valley. It was only a speck, disappearing into the sky above Granite Peak.

The sun shining into my eyes awakened me. O'kohome was curled up against me, half on top of me, keeping me warm. When I moved, a shower of water fell from the bush above me. Not that it mattered. I was already soaked through. "Come on, O'kohome," I said. "Wake up. We've gotta get out of here."

I looked at the rock in front of me. I could still picture the nighthawk sitting there. Had it been real? I laughed at the idea. Then I shook my head. A nighthawk! Not a great bald eagle. Not even a red-tailed hawk. No. A nighthawk. Not even a hawk, really. A little catcher of insects! Less than a foot long. What would Grandfather Wolf Runner say to that! Was I supposed to tell him? Or was it to be my secret? Grandfather had been on a vision, quest but he had never told me who his spirit helper was. But Chief Plenty Coups, greatest chief of the Crow people, was always talking about his guide, the chickadee. The chickadee? How could I complain about a nighthawk? I had hoped for something powerful: the grizzly, the eagle, something that could be an ideal, a real guide. I contemplated my ideas of the grizzly and the eagle. How did either of them ever help people? They hadn't helped me since I had been here. But every night the nighthawks were circling near my tipi catching mosquitoes. Maybe that was what I was supposed to do to, continuously help people in little inconspicuous ways. But how could a nighthawk guide me in bigger things? Then I remembered. A nighthawk zooming up toward Granite Peak had attracted my attention to it and gotten me to thinking about climbing it. When I started out to climb, a nighthawk was leading the way. And when I couldn't see a way up the cliffs, a nighthawk caused me to see the chimney, the crevice that led me to the top. It had been helping me all along, in little ways that I didn't even recognize!

The nighthawk was a much better symbol of the ways I could help my people. It would be much better to do little things for people every day, unobtrusively, even unnoticed, than to expect to do one great deed so that I would make a name for myself. I thought of Tobie shoveling the walks for an old man she didn't know, sending the dolls anonymously. Perhaps I could be like Ice, the great Cheyenne leader, who seemed to forget himself as he dedicated his life to helping our people. Grandfather had told me that if I expected to get help from the Great Father it could not be a one way street. I should expect to give back "as the sun gives light and the clouds give rain—to everyone." His statement hadn't meant much at the time, but now I understood. I would have to be more like the nighthawk.

I remembered what Grandfather had said, that I should keep, always, a reminder of the spirit helper, because it would be a reflection of the Great Spirit who would protect and guide me throughout my life. What could I take? I looked again at the rock in front of me. A small black rain-drenched feather with white stripes across it was lying on the ground near the rock. I picked the feather up and shook the water off. I reached inside my shirt and pulled out the little medicine bag that Tobie had made for me. I dropped the feather inside. Then I studied the beaded design on the front of the pouch. There was the diamond-shaped Morning Star, symbol of the Cheyenne. And in the middle another symbol: A horizontal line of black beads with one white bead near each end and one black bead above the line for a head, and two below for feet.

I heard a chirp and looked up. A nighthawk dipped and twisted in its climb above me, its long black wings with the white patch on the underside of each silhouetted against the blue sky. I looked again at Tobie's symbol. A nighthawk?

The Grizzly

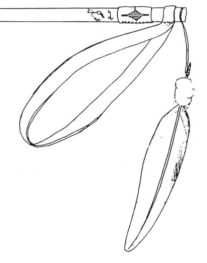

I sat in front of my tipi and carved a nighthawk on my coup stick. I took my time to make it a good carving so it would not only be a good memento of my vision, but also add to the beauty of the artifact. Grandfather Wolf Runner had told me I should record any really great events. The mountain climb had been my first, and I assumed my vision would be the last. Snow would be falling soon, and I would have to stick closer to camp.

There were only two more days of sunshine before the first big snowstorm. The air was still, not even a breath of breeze. I enjoyed the day sitting inside my tipi watching the huge flakes floating down.

The second morning I put on my snowshoes and strolled through the forest. A foot of snow was not enough for me to really need snowshoes, but I wanted to be accustomed to using them before the snow got deep. As I crossed some rabbit tracks I recalled walking with Tobie, and thought of her letter about walking in her snowshoes. I looked around and imagined Tobie's tracks leading into the forest.

From that morning on, every two or three days, a few more inches of fresh snow piled up. I banked some of it around my tipi to give it more insulation. With a good fire going it was cozy inside.

Now that the snow was deep and there were tracks to follow and study, hunting was more fun, but of course there was much less game. The marmots and ground squirrels were sleeping soundly and I assumed most of the bears were too, especially the mothers whose cubs would be arriving soon. The grizzly bear tracks that I found must be the tracks of a male. I had heard that the males would occasionally come out on warm days, and sometimes a big grizzly boar would stay out most of the winter.

My dog, O'kohome, and I didn't bring in a great deal of meat, but enough to keep from diminishing our supply of jerky and pemmican too rapidly. I was discovering how much food was required to keep us moving and warm. Any time that I got more game than we could eat, I could simply hang the extra meat in a tree, out of reach of the animals, and it would freeze solid. When mealtime came I could go out and cut off as much as I wanted. I also gathered a lot more wood. I didn't want to take any chance of running out during a blizzard.

These were happy days for me. I love to hike and explore, so while I hunted I searched out every nearby canyon and valley. I even climbed to the top of a couple of low mountains.

The snow kept piling up. For a while it was soft and fluffy. Even with my snowshoes I sank down a few inches. O'kohome tried futilely to chase a snowshoe hare. While he struggled through snow up to his chest, the snowshoe hare sprang across the top of the drifts as if it were on bare ground.

The sun shown brightly for a couple of warm days and the top snow melted. Then at night it froze into a hard crust. Now O'kohome could run happily across the top, but I was heavy enough to break through, so I still had to wear my snowshoes.

I was surprised to find some fresh deer tracks, as most of the deer had gone down to lower valleys. But I wasn't interested in hunting any more big game. We had all the smoked and dried meat we would need. I followed the trail just for the fun of it. As we came over a ridge and looked down, I saw the deer struggling across the meadow below, its belly deep in snow. It was apparently heading for a willow thicket where there would be plenty of brush to browse on.

Three coyotes came out of the timber and attacked. The deer could only flounder in the deep crusted snow while the coyotes ran on top. O'kohome acted like he wanted to join them, but I grabbed his harness and held on. "No, O'ko, if you interfere with their hunting, they'd probably gang up on you and kill you." Two ravens landed on the snow near the deer and sat waiting for the coyotes to finish their meal.

The next day it snowed another eight inches. Now I had to be careful where I went. That layer of fresh snow could easily slide on the crusted snow under it. If I crossed a steep mountainside, just my footsteps could bring down an avalanche.

I put another of my daily notches in my coup stick, then I counted the ones I had made. The end of November was nearly here. Thanksgiving time! It had been a full year since the history class had discussed Thanksgiving and the idea of this trip had begun. I had certainly learned a great deal in the intervening year. I wondered if any of the fellows in that history class besides Roger had done any thinking about their attitudes toward Native Americans.

Only three weeks left. I was beginning to get anxious to get back home. The last few weeks had been thoroughly enjoyable, but I was more and more convinced of the wisdom of the person who said, "Man was not made to live alone." Two men with a trap line for the winter, or a man and wife on a ranch, would be all right, but I wished I had someone to share all these good experiences with. Animals were good company, but they were not enough.

I decided to take all my food down out of the tree, and check to see just how much I had. That would tell me how much more hunting I should do. By now I knew pretty well what O'kohome and I would eat each day. I needed to be certain that I had enough, but no more. I didn't want to run out, but I didn't hanker to kill anything unnecessarily, or to waste any food. That was against my own principles, as well as all Native American traditions.

O'kohome was off hunting somewhere, so this was a good time to check my supply. He wouldn't be hungrily watching, expecting me to share some of the food. I untied the ropes and lowered the food. There appeared to be nearly enough to feed both of us for three weeks. We might want to go after another rabbit or two when we felt like it, but we could get along without them.

I sorted my food into three bundles. I tied my cornmeal and dried vegetables onto one of the three ropes, ready to pull up into the tree. The dried meat and fish made another, and I was just attaching my frozen fresh meat to the third when I heard a limb snap and looked up. A big grizzly, and I mean huge, was coming out of the timber. I stared at him and shouted, "What are you doing out here? Go back to your den where you belong!"

The bear stood up on his hind legs, stuck his nose in the air and sniffed. Then he dropped to all fours and headed directly toward me at a fast walk. I grabbed one of the ropes, the one tied to the dried meat, and pulled the bundle up as I backed away. But there wasn't time enough to tie it. I let go when I got to the end of the rope, and the bundle dropped right in front of the bear's nose. He tore into that bundle first, and gobbled most of it up before he started on the other two. All I could do was stand back and fume, and worry about how I was going to eat for the next three weeks.

When the grizzly finally left, I walked over and checked the damage. There was no pemmican or fresh meat left. I was able to pick as much jerky out of the snow as we would normally eat in a couple of days. Maybe if I stretched it out I could make it last twice that long—if I had vegetables. But there was only a tiny bit of corn meal left in the bottom of the sack. That grizzly bear certainly had a big appetite!

O'kohome came back a half hour later. I was hoping he would be carrying a rabbit, but he wasn't. "Where were you when I needed you?" I asked. He wagged his tail happily.

"Now we've got to do some real hunting."

He knew that word, "hunting," and danced around me.

"Look who was here while you were gone!" I pointed to a bear track. Usually when I showed him a track he would take off down the trail to investigate, but this time he stuck his tail between his legs and slunk back to me. Apparently he had already met a grizzly out there somewhere.

"I guess you don't care much for grizzlies! It's just as well. I'm not about to go hunting one, even if I would like to eat the one that gobbled up all our food." I got my bow and quiver of arrows and we went hunting, but we didn't see an animal all day.

I didn't eat anything that night or the next morning. I saved my food. I spent the day hunting porcupine. There had to be three somewhere nearby—the mother and two young ones that had visited me earlier. They don't move far, so they would each be in a tree somewhere within a half mile or so. I had been told that there used to be a law against killing porcupines because they are the only animal that a person lost in the forest can kill with a club. Porcupine meat had saved more than one life. Now maybe it would save mine. I walked through the forest methodically examining each tree from top to bottom.

I found several places where porcupines had eaten the bark off one side of a tree. I could tell the depth of the snow at the time by the height of the chewed bark. There were other trees where a porcupine had sat on a big limb, eating the bark above it. But no mater how hard I searched I couldn't see a porcupine. They must have each found a spot high in a tree where there were enough lower limbs to keep them hidden.

I even stayed out in the forest wandering around late into the night, hoping to hear some of the "porcupine talk." But they weren't talking—at least not near me. Maybe they don't talk in the winter when they're alone, I mused.

I finally became so cold and tired and hungry that I was forced to trudge back to my tipi. I kindled a small fire and huddled over it while I added a handful of snow to a little cornmeal and heated it. I cut up one small piece of jerky and added it. I ate slowly, giving O'kohome only a couple of tastes.

The next day I ranged farther. In the warm weather I had fasted for four days, but this wasn't summer. To keep warm and to have the strength to wade through the snow all day, my body needed a lot of food. I kept on looking for porcupine, but I also kept my eyes roaming, watching for any movement, any sign of life. There must have been grouse somewhere, but I couldn't find them. It would be miles up to where there were ptarmigan, and if I climbed there, I wasn't sure I could find them. They might have passages among the snow willows, deep below the drifts. O'kohome dashed off on the trails of two rabbits but didn't catch either one.

I remembered where to find the one small bunch of wild rose bushes in the valley. Only the tops were sticking out of the snow. Digging around through them, I found a half dozen small rose hips and ate them. I wished I hadn't done such a good job of picking them early in the fall. I went to the limber pine trees but all the cones were empty. I had no idea where the squirrels might have hidden the nuts.

I had never seen the area so devoid of animal tracks. I headed for the lower end of the valley hoping that a deer or elk might have stayed for the winter. There were tracks of one deer, but they were several days old. I found an elk trail that appeared somewhat fresher—only a day or two old—so I followed it until it went over a high ridge out of the valley. At the top of the ridge I had to turn back; it was nearly dark. Anyway, the elk was probably miles away. Fortunately, it is never totally dark when there is snow on the ground.

My tipi had never looked so good. I barely managed to build a small fire before I crawled into my caribou skins.

I lay there thinking. I certainly hated to give up and go home three weeks early, but that would be better than starving to death. I was already feeling the effects of not having enough food. I was tiring more easily. It required more fire to keep me warm.

At dawn I checked the little food I had left, and made up my mind. There was enough jerky for a day, but I would divide it into three parts and force myself to keep going for three more days: two to hunt and one to get out of the wilderness. But there was no point in staying in this valley. I'd take my caribou sleeping bag and head down into the valley below. That's where the deer and elk went for the winter. Surely some of them would stay there along Sioux Charlie Lake and the Stillwater River. They wouldn't all go down into the ranch land below. Today and tomorrow I would hunt. If I didn't find any meat, I would head out the next morning.

I hated the thought of killing a deer or elk that far away from camp and having to carry the meat several miles, mostly uphill, but at least if I got one I would have plenty to eat, and I could make more than one trip if necessary.

I checked my survival kit to be sure everything was there: my lighter, candle, copper wire, pad and pencil, space blanket, and a little three-inch-long, one-celled flashlight. Everything was there but my compass. I had been practicing using the mirror on the back of the compass for signaling and hadn't put it back. I didn't bother to look for it. I knew this valley thoroughly now. I wouldn't need it. Getting on my way was more important.

I folded the survival kit and a pot for melting snow and cooking into my sleeping bag. I put my knife on my belt, and slung my pack on my back.

I crossed the tracks of one lone deer. From the pointed hoofs I was almost certain it was a doe, but the tracks looked a day old. Any attempt to go up the valley to look for that deer would probably be futile, and would also take me farther away from the Stillwater Valley where there was a much better chance of getting game.

I was beginning to weaken from so much exertion with very little food. The distance to the lower valley seemed twice as far as before. I finally reached Sioux Charlie Lake and followed the shore down the valley. I stopped to cut some willow stems and began chewing the bark off as I walked. It had a stronger, more bitter taste than that of the snow willows on the mountaintop. I didn't know how much my stomach could take. I didn't want to add stomach troubles to my other problems.

High on the cliffs on the other side of the valley I could see some spots not quite as white as the snowbanks. I watched carefully and counted seven bighorn sheep: four bucks and three ewes. There was no chance of climbing up to them with the whole mountainside, except for the cliffs, buried in deep snow. Anyway, with their sharp long-distance vision, the bighorns were probably already watching me. They were not a potential source of meat.

There were some week-old elk tracks, but no tracks of deer.

The lake was frozen over, so I didn't even consider the possibility of fish, until I came to an area where the ice had been broken up. There was only a thin skin between the broken chunks, where the tracks of two moose came out of the lake. I followed them until I found that they were headed up into Grizzly Valley. I remembered the day that Jose, Roger, and I had gone up there and found my potential campsite; we had seen moose in the swampy area above the beaver dam. Maybe that's where these were headed. I tracked them a little farther. I was getting worn out. Could I make it up to that valley today? Probably not, but tomorrow?

I remembered the story told by one of the old men of the Cheyenne tribe—how his father had chased a moose for three days and finally run it down, as my grandfather had done with wild horses. I certainly was not in condition for that, but I had gotten within arrow range of the one up near Granite Peak. Maybe I could get close to these. If I didn't get a deer today, I would have to consider the possibility.

By the time I made it back to the lake I was worn out completely. I had to sit and rest for a while. Maybe I should just give up and head out, leave my tipi and supplies right where they were, then come back for them sometime before summer. I wouldn't have the strength to get down to the Woodbine trailhead today, but I could go part way, then get there tomorrow. There wouldn't be any one at the trailhead or campground in winter, but there were ranch houses and a mine a few miles farther down the valley where I might get help. Or maybe I'd still find a deer on the way down the valley. I forced myself to get up and struggle on down the lakeshore. I had become so used to my snowshoes that walking in them had seemed easy. Now they weighed a ton, and so did my sleeping bag.

I didn't see another big game track all the way to the lower end of the lake. There, the water tumbled over some very steep rapids and was not frozen. I started on downstream. At the bottom of the rapids was a wide pool. A flat rock ran along my side of the pool about a foot above the waterline. I climbed down to it. As I stepped onto the stone a huge trout rippled the water as he darted toward me into the dark shadows under the rock. I dropped to my stomach on the rock and looked down. All I could see under the rock was darkness. I had done some noodling for small fish in Lame Deer Creek. I pulled off my mittens

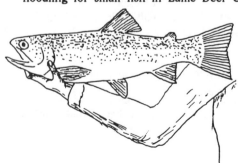

and reached down, moving my hands very slowly, down into the water and back under the rock, until I felt the fish. When I could feel him with both hands I clamped down. He flopped and struggled but I managed to hang on until I could get him on top of the rock and bang his head on it. The trout was as long as my arm from the tips of my fingers to my elbow.

O'kohome wagged his tail and looked happy for the first time that day. He had been following along, trying to hunt with me, struggling to keep up in the places where there was no crust on the snow. He was getting weak, too. He had been subsisting on less food than I was eating.

I realized that my hands and arms felt as if they were about to freeze. I dried my hands off the best I could and pulled my mittens on. There was no way I could warm my arms. My coat and shirt sleeves were soaked almost to my armpits.

I cut off a bite of raw fish for me and gave one to O'kohome. Then I broke some twigs and small dead limbs from the bottoms of the nearby pines and took them to the rock where I had caught the trout. I pulled my mittens off and took the lighter and candle from my survival kit. I tried to flick the lighter to start a fire but my hands were so cold and stiff I couldn't get it to work. I dropped it, and it slid almost to the edge of the rock. If I left it on the rock and it got cold, down near zero, the propane would thicken and it wouldn't work! I managed to get it picked up without knocking it into the water, then I moved away from the stream to put it into my pocket where it would stay warm.

I could eat the fish raw if I had to, but with my arms and sleeves soaking wet I was in danger of hypothermia unless I got a fire going. I managed to get my right arm out of the parka sleeve without taking the parka off, then I put my hand up under my left arm pit to warm it up. In spite of my fatigue, I danced around to try to produce a little body heat and get my circulation going.

After a few minutes I stuck my hand out from under my parka, picked up the lighter, and flicked it. To my great relief it flared up. With my mittened left hand I held the candle over it, then I held a bundle of small twigs over the candle flame. As soon as I had a fire going, I gathered some larger sticks to add to it.

I managed to dress out the trout with my mittens on. From my survival kit I took one of the pieces of fine copper wire that I carried for snaring rabbits. I used it to bind the trout to a willow stick and held it over the fire to roast. I put the tail end of the baked trout into my parka pocket for later. I ate the rest slowly, savoring the flavor; two bites for me, then one for O'kohome .

I finally got the sleeves of my shirt and parka almost dry, at least on the outside, and decided it was safe to move on. I felt so much stronger after the rest and the food that I gave up my intention of trying to head out of the wilderness today. Instead, I would climb up into Grizzly Valley where there might be both moose and elk.

The sun had already disappeared over the high mountains in the west and I could feel the air growing colder. I climbed up to the little cave where I had camped the night I shot the deer. I built a fire in the entrance and stacked up enough dead wood to last me all night. O'kohome and I shared the rest of the trout. I saved the piece of jerky I had planned to eat. Added to the one I planned for tomorrow it would make a small meal. By the time I went to sleep I was pretty well dried out.

The sun was shining brightly the next morning and I tried to be optimistic as I followed the moose tracks up into Grizzly Valley. Climbing over the downed timber and up the steep slope into the valley was much more difficult than it had been when I was stronger and there was no snow.

Hip-deep snow covered the swamp above the beaver pond, but two big bull moose were browsing on the willows at the upper end. They ignored me as I slowly approached them until I was almost within arrow range, then they started walking away. Their long powerful legs took them easily through the deep snow, and even walking on top with my snowshoes, I struggled to keep up.

I wasn't sure why I was following them. Mainly I was hoping they would lead me to other wild game, but I didn't see any other tracks, except those of the tiny voles, and here and there some bird tracks. I still had a license for a doe mule deer, but I didn't have one for a moose. I laughed at the thought of someone coming up here today to arrest me for killing one. I'd welcome them with open arms. They wouldn't let me starve. I thought I remembered something in the game laws about it being legal to kill an animal to save a life. Would this count? I didn't really think I could kill a moose with one arrow anyway. And if I killed one it would have to be with one arrow. Even without its huge antlers a moose could kill a man in seconds with his hoofs. I knew that an angry one was more dangerous than a grizzly bear. But maybe, just maybe, if I got in the right position, perhaps on a cliff above them . . . .

We passed the tree with the big rock beside it where I had first talked of camping, then the grizzly-marked tree. The flat rock was still on top of the big boulder beside it so I assumed my note was still there. I wished the boys had come up and found it and spent a weekend with me. Even better, they could have brought Tobie along! I wondered if she had ever come back from Peru.

About that time a few snow flakes hit me in the face. I had been so intent on following the moose that I hadn't even noticed when the clouds had hid the sun. Maybe it was the quick change in the weather that disturbed the larger of the two bulls. He suddenly turned around and faced me. He lowered his head, swung his huge antlers back and forth, and pawed the snow with one hoof. Then he took one step forward. I took a slow step backward, then another. I might die of starvation but that would be better than dying suddenly under the hooves of a moose! I almost panicked when he took two more steps toward me. As I backed away, the tail end of my snowshoe dug into the snow and I fell backward.

Terrified, I looked up expecting the moose to be almost on top of me, but he was standing watching me. As I floundered in the deep snow, trying desperately to get my snowshoes under me, he slowly turned around and walked away.

11

The Blizzard

A low moaning sound alarmed me. I looked up and the tops of the trees were swaying; then a blast of wind and icy snow crystals slammed me in the face. I headed across the valley fast. I tried to run, but I could only stagger forward against the wind. I wanted to get on the ledge that would take me around the ridge into my own valley and my tipi while I could still see to find it.

By the time I got to the ridge I couldn't see ten feet in front of me. I climbed up it and around some rocks. There, sure enough, was a ledge. "Is this the right one, O'kohome?" It must have been because O'kohome trotted ahead of me.

I crossed a steep snowbank and hoped I wouldn't start an avalanche. Then suddenly, O'kohome stopped. When I stepped up beside him I was looking down over a high cliff. I turned to the right and looked down again. I could see nothing below but swirling snow. To the left, cliffs ran straight up as far as I could see, which wasn't very far. This must be the dead-end ledge I had tried to follow when I first crossed over from Grizzly Valley to where I was camped. I couldn't see enough to know for sure. A blast of wind struck me from behind, and almost shoved me off the cliff. Now I knew I couldn't even count on the direction of the wind to tell me the way.

I turned and started back, watching carefully so I wouldn't go off the edge. I would have to go back into the valley, then up a couple of hundred yards, to get on the right ledge. I blindly walked up the valley to what I thought was about the correct location, and turned right. That should have put me on the ridge, but it didn't. The ground just gradually sloped upward. I must still have been going up the valley. I turned to the right again, but I didn't come to the ridge. The ground in front of me dropped off into a ravine. I could see nothing but white around me. There was nothing to indicate my location, or which direction I was going in.

I turned around. If I could follow my tracks back to where I had last seen the moose, I would at least know where I was, and I might be able to find my way. But the tracks before me were already half full of snow. By the time I walked a dozen steps the wind-blown snow had removed any hint of my tracks, and I knew I was totally lost. I had my survival kit. I always carried it, but this time there was no compass in it. How I wished I had taken time to find it!

O'kohome was following at my heels. "O'kohome," I said. "Go home." I motioned out ahead. He started off, and I struggled to keep him in sight. For a moment I was afraid that he thought he was to go home without me. Then he slowed down. He kept looking on all sides. Was he  headed for home, or did he think I was still hunting, and thus leading me in the opposite direction? Were we going somewhere or just walking in circles?

Now the white was turning to black. With the coming of night the temperature dropped dramatically. We had to find shelter of some kind. I struggled on. When the wind had first come up it had been blowing from the direction of my camp, so I kept walking into the wind.

Suddenly I ran up against a snowbank as high as my head. Apparently the wind coming over some rocks or a ridge had piled it into a deep drift, a cornice. I wondered if the part on top of the drift was packed hard enough to hold its own weight if I dug under it. If it was mostly old packed snow, it should be pretty solid. I took off one of my snowshoes and used it for a shovel to dig into the bank. I soon had a hole big enough to crawl into. I kept digging and piling the snow up behind me. I widened the hole enough for both O'kohome and me to sit down in it. I dragged in some pine boughs to sort of support the snowbank that was my roof. With my numb fingers it seemed as though it took me hours. I filled in the entrance until there was only a small hole for air.

I took off my pack, succeeded in untying the thongs that held the caribou hide sleeping bag folded into a pack, then struggled into it. I invited O'kohome inside and he managed to squeeze in although I had only made the sleeping bag big enough for one. Being together seemed to warm us both a little. I was certainly thankful for Tobie's beaver-fur cap that kept my head warm.

My famished body was so completely fatigued I could hardly move. After a little while I reached one arm out and searched the snow for the small bag that had been folded inside my pack. I found it and got out the small flashlight and two pieces of jerky I had saved the night before. I tore one in two and shared it with O'kohome. I ate the other.

After a while I was feeling almost comfortably warm. Was our body heat and our breath actually warming the air inside our ice cave, or was hypothermia deceiving me and just making me feel warm? I hoped it was the former. I pushed the sleeping bag down so I could get both arms out and dig the cave a little longer, so we could lie down. Now there was absolute silence except for O'kohome's breathing. Had the wind died, or was I just insulated from the sound by the snow?

I dozed and awoke and dozed again. This went on for hours. Finally I woke up, and realized a little bit of light was filtering through the snow in the front of the cave. I reached out and used the heel of my snowshoe to make a hole large enough to see out of. It wasn't much lighter outside than inside. The wind was still whistling and the cold air made its way in through the hole. I filled it in again, leaving only a tiny air hole.

I was famished, but my thirst was even stronger. I knew how foolhardy eating snow would be. More than one person had died of hypothermia from eating snow. How many calories of heat did it take to melt one gram of ice? I couldn't remember, but I knew it was a lot.

I sat there for what seemed like hours. I knew a healthy person could live a week or a lot more without food, if they weren't too active. It hadn't been hard to do it for four days on my vision quest. But I had been climbing mountains and wading snowdrifts for a week with hardly anything to eat. I didn't know how many more days I could live without food. But I did know that kidneys and other parts of your body could shut down permanently if you went many days without water. I hadn't had any since yesterday morning at the lake. I punched a larger hole and looked out again. The snow was coming down as hard as ever, but the wind had died down. I made a doorway large enough to crawl through, and crawled out. O'kohome followed me and I told him, "Go find us a rabbit. Go on. Hunt! Rabbit!"

O'kohome left and I looked around. I could still see only a few feet and had no idea where I was. If I started walking I could just as easily be walking away from home as toward it. One thing was certain. I was in new territory.

I started gathering small, dead tree limbs for firewood, making sure I remembered every tree that I passed so I could be sure to find my snow cave again. I also found enough small dry twigs and leaves under fallen logs and branches to use for tinder. With my pile of firewood and twigs collected, I began enlarging my cave. I added about four feet at the end. Then I took a little wood inside and began piling more snow in to close the entrance. At the end of the cave away from my sleeping bag I punched two holes about six inches across, an air hole at the bottom and a smoke hole at the top. Then I built a very small fire. I packed my cooking pot with snow and put it on the fire. I soon had a drink of water, and kept on melting more snow.

When I had quenched my thirst I was hungrier than ever. I tried chewing on some pine needles but that didn't work. I gave that up in a hurry. I wondered how far it was to the nearest willows.

It must have been three hours before I heard O'kohome's whine. I made an opening for him to come through. He practically dragged himself through the hole. How I wished I had some kind of food I could share with him.

Water dripped from the snow roof and almost put the fire out, but the end of the cave with my sleeping bag stayed dry. Hours passed and it began to get dark. I went out and brought in some bigger wood, enough to keep a flame going all night. I put the ends of four long sticks in the fire.

When I woke up the fire had burned down to a few coals. I was too tired and lethargic to do anything about it, but after a few minutes I decided I had to force myself. I leaned out and blew on the coals until I got a little flame, then pushed the four sticks in so the tips were again together over the burning coals, and went back to sleep. Every time I woke up and pushed the sticks in, I hoped it was morning and the sun would be shining. Finally morning did come, but the wind was howling again and I could barely find enough strength to face it and find a little more wood. I wandered around gathering dead limbs and also looking for something, anything, to eat. I remembered the long, cold winter on the ranch. Our horses had chewed bark off the cedar trees, and we burned the spines off the cactus so the cattle could eat it. There were no cedar trees or cactus plants up here. I dragged the wood back to my snow cave, crawled back inside and collapsed. I kept a tiny fire going. I quit worrying about eating. I was no longer hungry. The wind died down and the snow stopped coming down, but a heavy fog took its place. I still had no idea where I was. The day dragged by, and another night.

It had been light an hour or two before I finally got up the strength to sit up and look out. The wind had come up again and there was so much snow in the air that I could hardly see the nearest trees. I couldn't tell if it was snowing again or if the wind was blowing yesterday's snow. I knew I should get out and gather some wood, but I didn't have the strength to face that wind.

O'kohome looked mournfully up at me and just managed a couple of half-hearted wags of his tail. I turned away and started to cry. Then I turned again and looked at O'kohome. He lowered his head as if to hide it between his paws.

"No, O'kohome. I'm not thinking of eating you." I remembered the Cheyenne legend Grandfather Wolf Runner had told me, of the time the whole village had run out of food and was in danger of starving. A father told his son that tomorrow they would have to start eating their dogs. The boy's dog would be the first. The boy had gone for a walk with his dog, then sent it away, telling it to never come back. Then he had gone to each dog in the village, sending it away. When the people got up the next morning there were no dogs in the village, and the people went for a day without food. However, when they rose the second morning, in front of each tipi was a pile of rabbits and other animals—meat that the dogs had caught for them. That day the people had a meeting and decided that they would never again eat dogs except for very important occasions when they were honoring a man for a very brave deed. I looked at O'kohome again and said, "You didn't bring me food to save my life, but you tried your best!" Then I remembered the story of Packer, the prospector who had eaten his five companions when they had been lost in the Colorado mountains for five months one winter. I wondered how long I could hold out.

I sat in my snow cave and thought. My mood shifted from boredom to confusion, to frustration, to fear, to anger—anger at Tobie and Jose for encouraging me to come here—anger at myself for not having sense enough to get out as soon as the bear ate my food—anger at my Creator for allowing such a thing to happen to me. Why had it happened? Why had I not been able to find more food? I had done everything right, I thought. I had been well prepared, and for a while things had gone well. The deer had even come right to me. For a moment I almost forgot my consternation, remembering the humor of having to make a flying tackle to stop the deer from going into the lake. I wished Tobie and Jose could have seen that!

Tobie would have liked that. She liked action. I remembered something she had said the afternoon I was trying to decide whether to come up here. "I don't care how long I live, but I do want to live, really live. Too many people are afraid of life and they never really live. I'd rather be a fiery meteor streaking across the sky and ending up in a fiery blaze than be a sleeping planet that goes on forever." Well, I had been having a lot of experiences that my friends would never have, but I couldn't quite call this going down in a blaze of glory.

I wondered what Grandfather would have said about my tackle. Then I recalled his instructions when we talked about hunting. "We always thank the Creator for bringing the deer. Then we thank the spirit of the deer for sacrificing itself to supply the necessities of life for us. If you don't show your appreciation for each deer you harvest, don't be surprised if no other deer ever comes to you." I had been so excited when I killed my deer that I hadn't remembered Grandfather's teachings. I probably wouldn't have prayed anyway. That was the old way. But I had said I would make this trip the old way. Wasn't my heart in it? I was sure it wasn't just for show. I had really wanted to prove that I could do it—to myself most of all. Then why hadn't I done it completely?

It had been a long time since I had actually prayed. What would I say anyway? I guess I could tell God, Ma'heo'o, the Creator, how unfair it was that everything had turned against me, that all the animals stayed away and I was about to starve. And I could ask Him to get me out of this alive and well. That's what I thought I'd say, but when I started to talk aloud, that's not what came out. I couldn't blame Him for my spreading all my food out where the grizzly could get it. He didn't send the grizzly. Or even if He did there was a reason, maybe a good one. He wasn't the one who decided I should stay when I had no food. But I guess I could ask for help.

What could I say to some far off Something, who probably wouldn't even hear me or care? Strangely, when I started talking I felt as if I weren't alone. It seemed as if someone was right there with me. When I started to ask for help, I asked for help in being more appreciative. I said how thankful I was for all the wonderful experiences I had this fall, for all that I had learned, for the self-confidence and inner strength I had gained, the friends who had helped me get here, even for the students in my class who had made me so angry that I had accepted their challenge. I was going to go on and ask for help, but what I asked for was the determination, the courage, and inner strength to do whatever was necessary to do my absolute best, and for the courage to accept whatever that led to.

I opened my eyes and looked around. Everything was the same, yet it seemed different. The place and the blizzard no longer seemed frightening. I was at peace. Why hadn't I let my whole autumn be a spiritual experience? That was the old way. To my ancestors, every day was a spiritual experience.

I remembered the night that Tobie and I had sat in the library and talked about being prepared for this trip. She said there were only four things needed for survival food, water, heat, and determination. "Call it courage," she had said.

Well, right now, I didn't have any of them! What would she say to that! I knew what she would say, what she had said that night. "Deaths in the wilderness are nearly always blamed on three things: starvation, dehydration, or hypothermia. But usually the real cause is giving up. The ones who survive in the really bad situations are the ones that have the determination to do it. Anyone can be prepared for the first three, but most of the people I know wouldn't have the determination. You have it. I can see it in your eyes."

I remembered what Grandfather had said. He had told me this was my challenge, my opportunity to prove my manhood, my bravery, as they did in the old days. I looked at the snow and ice that surrounded me, at the almost dead fire beside me, and I said aloud, "All right Tobie, you win. And you too, Grandfather."

I struggled to get out of my sleeping bag. It seemed to take me forever to tie my snowshoes on. I rested a minute before I punched a hole in my snow wall and crawled through. The drifts were a foot deeper than when I arrived. The wind had slacked a little, but the snow was still coming down. I laughed at myself when I tried to stand up and almost fell into a drift. I grinned when I thought of the expression Grandfather would have on his face if he saw me now, the strong, conquering warrior returning from his challenge, proving his manhood. What a laugh.

I could hardly walk, let alone go out and hunt for more firewood, but I did it. I wondered if I should be trying to walk out of these mountains instead of gathering wood to stay here. But I had no idea which way to go. Going downhill would get me out of the mountains—in a few days. A ridiculous idea.

It took me a long time to gather enough wood to last another day and night. As I finally crawled back into my den dragging my wood, O'kohome greeted me with a couple of thumps of his tail but he didn't move or try to get up.

I blew on the coals and got a little flame going, then added enough sticks to melt some snow in my little pot. I let it heat until it was hot, then I drank it, pretending it was an herbal tea. It warmed my stomach. I already had an inner warmth that I hadn't felt before. I spent the afternoon thinking of all the places I had hoped to get to sometime, and the adventures that I dreamed of. I wanted to always be going to new places, doing new things, but as Tobie had said in her letter, it was hard to leave old friends and the land of which you had become a part. I thought about dying. What would that be like? Maybe that would be the greatest adventure of all—going into a completely unknown land. I crawled into my sleeping bag, pulled O'kohome in with me and relaxed. I ached all over.

When I opened my eyes my fire was completely out, but it was surprisingly light in my little snow cave. I reached out and punched a hole in the wall. The sun was shining brightly. I made the hole larger so I could see the deep blue sky. I put the survival kit and pot on my fur sleeping bag and folded it into a square pack. I dragged it outside and put it on my back before I tied on my snowshoes. I almost forgot to pick up my bow and arrows.

With O'kohome following behind, getting some benefit from my packed snowshoe tracks, I went downhill. Before long the valley I was in led into another larger one, and I could see mountains that told me where I was. I had gone up a side valley to the east of the big valley that I called Grizzly Valley—the opposite way from my camp. I had to cross Grizzly Valley and a high ridge to get to my camp, but I knew that once I reached it, one more piece of jerky and a little bit of cornmeal were waiting for me. They might give me enough strength to get out of these mountains.

I should have been able to cross Grizzly Valley in an hour, but with frequent rests it took me all morning. With all the strength I could muster I finally managed to climb up to the right ledge to take me into the next valley and my tipi. I started down into the valley, head down, watching where I was going, thinking about nothing except trying to put one foot in front of the other.

A black bird zoomed across in front of me. A nighthawk? This time of year? I still don't know if it was a nighthawk or some other bird. As I raised my head to see, it was disappearing over the ridge above me. But if it hadn't been for the bird, I would not have been looking up at the top of the ridge when the head rose above it. Two big ears and the head of a mule deer doe. She kept coming till her whole body was in sight. Instead of the big leaps a mule deer uses when she is in a hurry, she was walking, struggling through snow clear to her belly. She must have been tired, too. She stopped on the top of the ridge and looked down at me. I turned and pushed down on my dog's neck. "Lie down, O'kohome. Stay. Be still." He was glad to lie still and rest as I started up the hill.

I didn't walk directly toward the deer. I didn't want to alarm her. I headed for a spot about a hundred yards below her. I was so excited I almost forgot how tired and weak I was. It must have taken fifteen minutes for me to reach a place below her, but she didn't move an inch. I walked on past, then I turned and walked back, still not walking directly toward her, but nearer. I stopped less that a hundred feet from

her. She was still standing unmoving, with her ears cocked forward, watching me intently. I turned, slowly, nocked an arrow, and carefully raised my bow. The arrow arched up and dropped, struck right in her upper chest where I had aimed. She leaped forward in one big leap and fell. I climbed up to her. She was lying sprawled out, obviously dead, the snow in front of her turning a bright crimson.

I pulled out my red bandana handkerchief and coiled it around the top of the deer's head like a crown. Then I squatted in the snow beside her and thanked her spirit for sacrificing itself for my needs, and the Spirit of all of Nature for providing for me.

I turned to call O'kohome, but he was already right behind me. He stepped forward and started licking at the red snow. It was all I could do to get the doe turned over enough to dress her out. As her entrails spilled out onto the snow I cut out the liver, then cut off two fist-sized chunks of it. I handed one to O'kohome and began cutting the other into bite size chunks and eating them. By the time I finished that and had cut off one hind leg, I was feeling stronger. I hoisted the leg onto my shoulder and headed for my tipi.

It wasn't long before I had a hot fire blazing in the middle of my tipi and a chunk of venison roasting. The heat reflected down from the slanted sides and warmed the whole inside. I got out my coup stick and cut four notches. I cut them a little deeper than the others, as I had the day I climbed Granite Peak. I laughed about thinking this morning that I would be on my way home tomorrow. No way was I going home before the day Roger was to pick me up!

When O'kohome and I finished eating, I really wanted to lie down and rest a few hours, but I knew I had to bring back the rest of the deer meat. If I had left it out there all night, coyotes or wolves or a mountain lion would probably have eaten it all. I hitched O'kohome to the dogsled, and together we pulled it across to the deer and hauled it back. By the time the carcass was hung up in my food tree, the moon was up. I felt as if there were a hand in mine as I thanked the Great Father for all that life had to offer me.

12

Missing

I crawled out of my caribou robes and pushed aside the door flap of my tipi. A full moon flooded the whole snow-covered valley. This might be my last opportunity to enjoy these mountains by moonlight. I pulled on my fur boots and attached my snowshoes.

O'kohome danced beside me. I glanced back at the big prints of my snowshoes, and remembered Tobie's letter about making big Tobie tracks. I put my imagination to work and whispered, come on Tobie, walk with me.

The tracks of a rabbit led me across the valley. The sudden end of the trail and the marks of a bird's wing tips in the snow on each side told me something had enjoyed a meal that night. I thought the distance between the wing tips was about right for the great horned owl. I'd have to watch more closely the shape of the wing tips of the hawks and owls as they flew over.

The full moon was near the western horizon and the long shadows of the tall pines streaking across the snow gave the whole valley a feeling of magic. This was a spiritual time, a time when it felt as though I, the animals, and all of nature were one. The days since the blizzard had provided many hours to relax, to dream, to contemplate. The inner peace I had felt that last night in my snow cave had come back often, and the quiet stillness of this night brought to me a feeling of harmony with all that surrounded me. But I recalled that there had also been days when I had such a lonesome feeling that I was tempted to just pack up and go home. Two-and-a-half months alone had been a long time. I was getting anxious to return home, to see my family, and my friends.

These last days had provided some wonderful memories, but they had also given me plenty of time to contemplate my own life. I remembered how hesitant I had been when I moved to Billings and started senior high. Afraid to talk to people because I might be rejected. And I recalled the difficulty I had making up my mind about this trip. New Year's Eve, the last time I had seen Tobie, she had told me I was afraid to really jump in whole-heartedly and participate fully in anything because I was afraid it might be taken away from me. During these last weeks I had made up my mind that from here on I would put my whole heart into each activity, knowing that, whether I succeeded or not, each struggle could be an adventure, and an opportunity to learn.

The full moon set behind the mountains which meant that it was about six o'clock in the morning, but at this time of the year the sun wouldn't rise for another two hours. I watched the Morning Star slowly 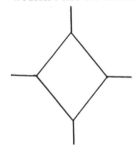 rising above the eastern horizon. That star was the symbol of the Cheyenne people. It could be my symbol, too. I sang out the words to a song we had learned at senior high, "This is my quest, to follow that star, no matter how hopeless, no matter how far!" And I remembered the lesson of the nighthawk, that finding many little ways to help would benefit my people more than any one, big daring act. I was now ready to find new ways to help my people. And that would take knowledge. My time here in the wilderness was about to end, but it had readied me for another kind of adventure. If I approached it with the right attitude, education would be an adventure, too? The time was coming soon when I would no longer be alone, and I was glad. Aristotle said it long ago "Without friends no one would choose to live." Aloneness had taught me how valuable friends were, how important each individual could be.

As I crossed the creek on my way back to the tipi, the sunrise gave the snow-covered mountain tops a crimson hue. I took a few minutes to watch two river otters having fun sliding down an icy snowbank into an open hole below some rapids. They ignored me and went running back up to slide again. I knew that life was not easy for the otters, who were facing a cold winter and a scarcity of food. Yet they always had time to play, to thoroughly enjoy life. I had been told that they always chose lifetime partners and were loyal to their mates till death. I waved goodbye to the otters as I started on. I was going to miss the animals. How many lessons we humans could learn from them! The old Cheyennes must have been right when they said that every animal had a spirit, a soul, the same as we do.

I stopped at my food tree and cut off two big slices of venison and a little bit of liver. I had been saving the liver, eating just a bit each day to make it last. Since I no longer had dried fruits or vegetables, it was my only supply of vitamins. Although my ancestors had never heard of vitamins, they knew having liver in the wintertime was important to keep them feeling healthy and strong.

While my breakfast cooked I carved one more notch in my coup stick. I counted to be sure. Yes, tomorrow was the day I was to meet Roger. I wondered if Jose would come with him. Or Tobie? I wondered if Tobie had come back from Peru. A lot of things could have happened in the three months I had been gone. I wondered if she ever thought of me.

Since the trail to Woodbine was nearly all downhill, I didn't need to start down till tomorrow morning. O'kohome wouldn't need much help from me pulling the dog sled. If I took down my tipi at dawn, I could make it to the trailhead in one day. Roger wouldn't expect me till evening.

On one of my lonesome days, I had packed everything except the tipi so I didn't have much preparation to do today. That left me free to take one more walk around the valley, recalling all the things I had done while I was here. I wouldn't have much time for contemplation once I was back in the rush of city life. I started up the valley toward Granite Peak, totally white now except for the granite cliffs near the top.

A chip of bark fell in front of me as I walked under a big ponderosa pine. I looked up and saw a porcupine sitting on a high branch, gnawing on the trunk of the tree. "Where were you when I really needed you?" I asked. "Oh well, maybe you can save someone else's life."

I wandered far up my side of the valley, then turned and came down the other side. When I was about at the spot where the ledge led across to Grizzly Valley, I saw tracks crossing ahead of me, big tracks. I hurried to examine them. They were definitely snowshoe tracks, but I hadn't been in that spot for several days. They couldn't be mine! No, the snowshoes were a little different, and they weren't quite as large as mine. "Tobie tracks," I said, remembering Tobie's letter about snowshoeing. How I wished that they really were Tobie tracks! But whose could they be? No one else had been in this valley all fall! Maybe Roger or Jose had come to meet me. But why wouldn't they have come together? Maybe I had miscounted, and I was a day late going out to meet them!

I followed the tracks, hurrying to catch up with whoever it was. I didn't think it could be Roger because the tracks weren't deep enough. Whoever it was, was lighter than me! The tracks led across the valley, toward my camp. As I hurried toward the tipi the rawhide door swung up and someone stepped out.

"Tobie!" I shouted. I ran toward her. I don't know if she intended to greet me with a hug, but she couldn't get out of this one!

"Tobie! Boy, am I glad to see you! But what ... what are you doing here?"

"Come inside and sit down, I've got a lot to tell you. Have you seen Jose?"

"Jose? No! Not since he and Roger dropped me off three months ago."

"Well, Jose is lost. They've been searching for him."

"Lost! Up here?"

"Yes. He and Roger came up to see you. Skipped school on Friday and thought they would spend a couple of days with you. They wanted to see your campsite. And maybe they were a little concerned about you after that big storm. Biggest one in several years."

"Yes, I know! But what happened to them?"

"They got separated somehow. I haven't heard the details. I think Roger hunted for Jose for a day, then came back and called Search and Rescue. There was a snow storm the night Jose got lost and it covered all their tracks. They've had thirty or forty people searching for the last three days."

"But how did you find my camp? None of the searchers have been here!"

"I didn't know about the search until last night's newscast. I dashed right over to talk to your mom. She gave me the map you had made to show her where you would be. I headed out this morning long before daylight. I left Mom's car at the searchers' camp at Woodbine and followed your map. The new map on your message rock told me where to find you. Am I glad to see *you're* okay anyway! When they didn't find Jose, or you either, I was scared. I felt responsible!"

"But why didn't Jose and Roger find me?"

"I don't know. It's a mystery to me. The instructions were clear enough. But there was another large pine with a big rock beside it, just about like your message rock, about a half mile below it. There were tracks of searchers around there, and a canvas bag full of stuff. I figured the searchers had left it. I thought first that might be your message rock, but there was no flat rock on top. Maybe Jose and Roger thought that was your campsite, and so they never found your message."

"Yes," I said, "I know the rock. That could easily be what happened. But how'd they get separated? Didn't Roger say?"

"I don't know. I didn't talk to Roger. I pulled in to the trailhead at daylight this morning. Roger was already out with a group, searching. There were still people milling around. I talked to some. They said the group would be searching all day today, but they thought if he wasn't found by tonight, Search and Rescue would conclude he couldn't still be alive, and they would call off the main search. Some of the individual searchers might stay longer. I just took your map and headed out."

"Did you tell the searchers where you were going?"

"No. I didn't know when I'd be back and I didn't want anyone to think I was lost and start searching for *me*. I knew I'd be all right. I've got my down sleeping bag in a Goretex cover that's made for climbs like McKinley or Kilamanjaro, and I have food for at least five days." She pointed to her pack on the other side of the tipi.

"No one knows where you are?"

"Just Mom. And I told her not to worry for at least five or six days."

"What did she say about that?"

"She wasn't happy!"

I wondered why none of the searchers had found my valley. I had been around it both yesterday and today, and there were no tracks except Tobie's.

Tobie said she saw searcher's tracks going up along the rocks and cliffs on this side of Grizzly Valley. "They probably didn't find the ledge you used to cross over into this valley and thought Jose couldn't possibly get over the ridge on snowshoes."

We talked it over and agreed we weren't going to give up till we found Jose. We would spend one day searching this valley, then go over beyond Grizzly Valley, to the one where I had waited out the blizzard.

"There's just one problem," I said. "I'm supposed to meet Roger tomorrow, and if I don't show they'll think I'm lost, too."

"You'll have to go to the meeting point tomorrow. Let them know you're okay. We need to know if Jose has been found, anyway."

"We'll go." I told her. "I'm not leaving you alone!"

"Oh yes you are. I can be searching while you're gone. We can't waste two days. Anyway, someone has to be here at your tipi every night, just in case Jose finds his way here. But I don't think you can make it there and back in a day!"

"I could start at daylight and be out in three or four hours with the dog sled. Most of the way is downhill, so O'kohome could pull the sled easy. I'll ride the back of the runners and run when I need to. Then I can run behind and push when we're on the level along Sioux Charlie Lake. We should be able to make it back by dark, if we don't wear out completely."

"Go now, this afternoon. That way you can get a night's sleep and start back fresh in the morning. I'll be searching while you're gone. Maybe Roger will come back with you." She grinned and winked at me as she added, "And I'll have a good hot dinner to welcome you home."

I didn't want to take a day and a half out from the search, and I definitely didn't want to leave Tobie. I hoped she hated that as much as I did. But I had learned a year ago that when Tobie makes up her mind, you can't force her to change it.

As I was leaving, Tobie said, "Flint, please don't tell them I am up here. It'll just complicate things. My life is my own business."

Staying overnight meant I had to take my sleeping bag, but I would have had to take it anyway for safety. The trip out of the valley was a lot harder than I had said it would be. It had seemed all downhill when I walked it, but I forgot about the places I had to climb away from the creek because of cliffs, and the logs that I would have to lift the sled over. But I did make it out before dark.

When I found Roger, he had worn himself out completely, and had developed a cough and a wheeze. The emergency medic who was there said he was not to leave camp the next day, so I would be going back alone. I asked Roger how he and Jose had become separated.

"We camped by the grizzly tree and the big rock where you were supposed to be camped. There was no note and the flat rock you were going to put it under was gone, but then it had been almost three months so we figured someone else had found it."

"It was still there. T . . ." I remembered just in time that Tobie didn't really want anyone to know she was there. "At least I left one. Maybe you found the wrong tree and rock. There was a similar one lower down in the valley."

"Well, the next morning we walked around the valley looking for you and your tipi, but we couldn't find you. That afternoon, Jose said he was going farther up the valley to look for you, but I was worn out and decided to stay at camp and get some rest. Jose never came back. I searched for him all the next day. Then I hiked out and called Search and Rescue. I left all our stuff except my sleeping bag right there by the tree for Jose, but I guess he never did get back to it. I sure hope you can find him."

"We will," I said. "We've got to!"

13

The Rescue

The moon was still up when I started back. It was much harder going up hill. I was thankful that I had O'kohome to help pull the sled. And I was glad to have it instead of a heavy pack. When we reached Sioux Charlie Lake, we stopped for a rest. I kept thinking about Jose. If he had gone on farther up Grizzly Valley after he left Roger, maybe he found my message rock. Then he would have headed over the ridge toward my camp. But why didn't he get there? I knew the searchers had covered Grizzly Valley pretty thoroughly, but I couldn't help thinking maybe, just maybe, I could find a clue that they didn't. By now I knew the area better than any of them could. So instead of heading directly for my camp, I decided to go up Grizzly Valley, then across the ridge and back to camp. It was harder going because of the downed timber I had to lift the sled over, but by late morning I found the canvas bag full of stuff that Roger had left where they camped. Sure enough it was at the lower grizzly-marked tree.

I went up the valley to my message rock. My note was still under the flat rock on top where Tobie had found it. If Jose had seen it he would surely have either gone back to get Roger, or gone west over the ridge to my camp. I could also see the entrance to the valley that turned off to the east, where I spent the blizzard. If he got turned around in the snowstorm, he could have gone that way, as I did. But surely the searchers would have covered that valley since it was easy to get into. Tobie and I could search it again if we didn't find Jose in my valley.

I started to angle up the valley toward the spot where I could get onto the ledge that would take me around the ridge toward camp, but straight across the valley was the ledge that only went half way. Jose could have taken that one. I went straight across to check it out. There were snowshoe tracks on it showing that the searchers had been there yesterday. No use my checking too. But I felt that I just had to make sure. I unhitched O'kohome from the sled before we started along the dead-end ledge. I pointed ahead and said, "O'kohome, find Jose."

O'kohome sprang forward, but instead of following the ledge, he dashed down the ridge pursuing a snowshoe hare.

I yelled, "No. Not a rabbit! Find Jose." But O'kohome ignored me and disappeared into the timber.

As I walked the ledge I kept looking down over the cliffs to the right and up the mountain to the left and calling Jose's name, although I didn't expect a response. I reached the end of the ledge and looked down over the cliff. I studied the snow-covered area below. There was not even a sign of a track. I was about to turn and head back to the sled when I heard O'kohome's yelp. It wasn't the bark he would use to greet a stranger, but a yelp he would use if he wanted in the house on a cold night. I laughed. "No way, O'kohome. If you want up on this ledge you'll have to find your own way. I'm not coming down to help you."

O'kohome yelped again from the same spot. I stepped out of my snowshoes and climbed out onto some rocks so I could get a better view below the cliffs. "Where are you O'ko?"

He whined and I climbed out to another rock. There, below me, I spotted the dog. He was digging at a snow bank. "O'kohome, if you think you can dig a marmot out, you're out of luck." Then I thought, maybe, just maybe. . . Excited by the thought that it might be Jose, I hurried back to a spot where I could climb down over the cliffs. As I climbed down, with my snowshoes on my back, I thought, if it is Jose under that snowdrift, he must be dead. I dreaded the thought of finding his frozen body. Whoa! Wait! Maybe that's a bear he's after! I cautiously stepped around the trees and looked at the dog tracks leading to the snow bank.

O'kohome had dug a hole and was clear inside, except for his tail. I half expected to hear some yelping and see him tearing out of there, running to me, with a bear a foot behind. I stopped a moment. The tail waved then disappeared. I ran to look in. O'kohome's tail was wagging and two arms were around his neck. The face he was licking was Jose's.

There were only about two feet of air space around Jose, not enough space for me, so when I forced my way into the hole O'kohome had dug, the snow walls and roof caved in and covered all three of us. I tried to brush enough away to see Jose's face. He looked at me with a blank stare.

"Jose, it's me, Flint. Are you all right?"

"Uh-huh."

"How long have you been here?"

He shrugged his shoulders.

I brushed away some more snow and found that the aluminum foil space blanket I had given him for his survival kit was partly wrapped around him. I cleared away the snow and dragged him free then tried to help him stand up. He gave a yelp of pain and fell back against the snow bank. He waved an arm in a "What's the use?" kind of gesture.

I tried to talk with Jose as I brushed away the snow and raised him into a sitting position, but I couldn't get any coherent answers. "Come on, O'kohome. We've got to get the sled," I called as I turned and ran.

It took some maneuvering through the rocks and trees, but I finally got the sled to where Jose still sat. With a little half-conscious help from him, I tried to get him into my caribou hide sleeping bag, but when I started to lift his left leg he moaned in pain. I moved it carefully and could hear bones grating. I broke two dead limbs from a tree into two pieces that would reach from his knee to the bottom of his foot, then used my scarf and a piece of rope to bind them, one on each side of his leg. I finally got him into the sleeping bag and dragged

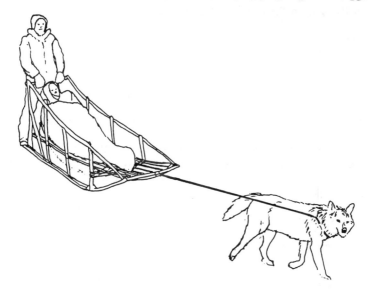

it onto the sled. I knew it was critical that I get help for Jose as soon as possible, but it took about three hours to maneuver the sled back into Grizzly Valley, up the valley to the right ledge and over the ridge toward my tipi. In all that time Jose uttered only a couple of half-distinguishable sentences.

As soon as we came within sight of the tipi, Tobie stepped out of the door and waved. I pointed to the sled and called, "It's, Jose."

In seconds Tobie had her snowshoes on and came running. She grabbed hold of the rope and almost left me behind, pulling the sled toward the tipi.

After we got Jose inside, close to the warm fire, Tobie began checking him over, trying to get him to talk as she pulled off his boots and examined his feet.

"You go about that like a doctor, not a high school student," I commented.

"I got a little training," she said. "Ski patrol. I don't think anything's frozen badly enough that they'll have to amputate or anything like that. We can improve on that splint you did, but that can wait. I'm sure he's dehydrated, too. But the thing that really scares me is hypothermia. If we don't get his body temperature raised pretty fast, he's not going to make it! Fill your water bottle with water from that pan I've got on the fire. It should be warm enough."

Tobie took a sip of the water to be sure it was hot but not enough to scald. Then she made certain Jose was conscious enough to swallow and forced him to drink as much as he could. "That'll help his dehydration," she said, "and warm him a little from the inside. But we've got to get him warm from the outside, too."

"I'll bring in more wood, and build a hotter fire."

"That won't do it. Once a person's body shuts down and quits producing its own heat, you just don't get enough transfer of heat from the air to raise its internal temperature. There are only two things that will help."

"What's that?"

"Put him in a tub of warm water. We don't have that. Or . . ." She hesitated.

"Or what?"

"Put naked body against naked body. Come on, we've got to strip him—down to his shorts."

As she pulled Jose's wool shirt off, I asked, "Wouldn't that wool shirt help him? It's a good heavy warm one."

"You can't get much heat to his body through a wool shirt. If you could, it wouldn't keep you warm. No. You have to have bare skin against bare skin to get a lot of heat transfer."

We got him stripped and then laid him on two layers of caribou hides with the fur side toward him, then we put another layer, and my sleeping bag on top. "All right," Tobie said. "Get your clothes off. I mean everything! And get in there with him." She turned her back and went to the door. She pushed the door flap aside just long enough to let O'kohome in. "Get in front of him, with your back to him and his arms around you. You've got to get heat to his tummy and his chest."

"Wouldn't it be better if I got behind him, so I could use my arms?"

"I'll take care of his back. Just tell me when you're in place."

Tobie checked our positions, then said. "That's great. Now just look at your coup stick there against the wall and think about how much spiritual help and inner warmth he needs to get well."

A couple of minutes later a hand reached around from behind and gave my arm a squeeze. Tobie retracted the arm, raised up and patted the top of the caribou hide above Jose. "Come on O'kohome. You can sleep here. A little heat from the top, too, might help." She settled back down and said, "You might as well get some sleep too, Flint. We'll be here a long time."

After all I had done, I needed some rest, but I didn't think I was likely to go to sleep.

When I woke up it was dark outside. Tobie was dressed except for her boots and was kneeling beside the fire blowing on the coals. When she saw me move she said. "I promised you a good hot dinner when you got back, and I don't even have a good fire going. While I go cut a few slices of venison, help Jose into your sleeping bag."

As she went out the door I turned over and asked. "Jose, are you all right?"

"Uh-huh. Good enough to like being hugged." He put his hands out like he was shoving me away, and added, "But not by you!" We both laughed.

When Tobie came back in, she tore apart my little fireplace to get two hot stones. She wrapped them in my spare shirt and Levis, and put them in the sleeping bag with Jose. We'll put new hot ones in later tonight," she told him.

I offered to put my Cheyenne willow backrest behind Jose so he could sit up, but he felt a little dizzy and nauseated when he tried. He wasn't able to eat much of the stew that Tobie made with the venison and some dried vegetables from her pack, but he slurped up the broth and some hot green tea.

Jose's mind was still somewhat befuddled, but he did finally remember enough to tell us how he had gotten to where I found him. "It was fairly warm when I left Roger, but he insisted I should take my down jacket along anyway. So I put on my pack with my jacket and the survival kit you insisted I make last summer. I started up the valley to see if you might be camped farther up than where we had looked. I took a different route from the one Roger and I had taken earlier and I found the right tree with the bear scratches on it. Then I knew we had camped in the wrong place. I read your message and decided to try to find the route over to your camp before I went back and got Roger. I found the ledge that was supposed to take me around the mountain to your place, but about that time a sudden snowstorm came up and the wind was blowing snow in my face, so I put my warm jacket on. I must of got off the ledge somehow and I came to a straight drop-off. I was going back and forth there trying to see through the blinding snow and find the right trail when I slipped. I tried to grab hold of the rocks as I went over the edge but I just banged against them all the way to the bottom. When I tried to get up I knew my leg was broken. It hurt so bad when I tried to move, and the other knee was banged up, and my wrist felt sprained. I couldn't hardly crawl. I got the whistle out of my survival kit and kept blowing it. There was a big snowbank a little ways above me. I remembered you saying how you could make a snow cave. So when the sun set, and it started gettin' colder, I managed to use my arms to drag myself up to the bank, then I used my snowshoe to dig a hole. I wrapped the space blanket from my survival kit around me and hoped that might get me by till morning."

When we asked about what had happened during the last four days, he looked puzzled, "Didn't Roger tell you about it? About our coming up to see you?"

Tobie told him, "Yes, we know all about that. We mean the four days since your accident."

Jose looked more puzzled than ever. "Four days? Wasn't that yesterday?"

With some Aleve from Tobie's survival kit to relieve the pain of his broken leg, Jose was ready for some rest. Tobie unrolled her sleeping bag and told me, "I'll take the left side of the tipi, the women's side. Jose already has the men's side and your sleeping bag. I guess that puts you in your caribou robes at the back. That's where the head of the clan is supposed to be anyhow."

"Sorry there isn't room for two to sleep side by side without burning a sleeping bag." I said.

"It's better this way, anyway. If we were too close we wouldn't get as much sleep. Besides, I want you as a friend for a lifetime, not just tonight. Just sleep with your head my way. We'll get our heads together."

"That's what we always do," I said. "Just our heads."

Together, we lifted Jose and the sleeping bag and moved him to the men's side of the tipi. Then I put my caribou robes across the back. I brought in enough wood to keep a warm fire going all night, and piled it at Tobie's

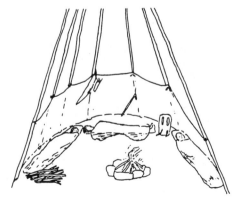

feet. I put three pieces on the fire. Tobie made sure Jose was as comfortable as possible. When the fire was burning well, Tobie and I crawled in, with our heads just a few inches apart.

Tobie reached out and touched my head. I reached up and took her hand. We lay on our backs with our hands between our heads, holding hands as we talked.

When the conversation lagged, Tobie gave my hand a tight squeeze, and pulled her hand away. A few minutes later she flipped over and scooted far enough out of her sleeping bag so she could raise up and look straight down into my face. A scarf held her hair back. Her face was radiant in the flickering firelight. She said in a low soft voice, "I got a package in the mail, but there was no name, and no return address. I took it to Peru with me. Inside were three Hershey's kisses, three hugs, and three dates. They tantalized me some evenings when I was alone. But they helped take away some of the loneliness. The hugs were a great idea. I like hugs. But the kisses—I shouldn't have gotten them. So I'm going to return those kisses."

I reached up to pull her head down to mine, but she scooted away into her sleeping bag adding, "Maybe!" She pulled the cover up over her head and added, "Someday!"

Jose was able to eat a good hot breakfast in the morning, and while Tobie packed up and put the fire out, I put the caribou hides in the sled, to provide a comfortable place for Jose.

"We ought to get out of here as quickly as we can," I told Tobie, "to be sure we can get him to a doctor today. Give me a hand and it'll only take a few minutes to get the tipi down."

"Leave it up," she said. "We'll need it next weekend."

"Next weekend?"

"Yes, when we come back after the rest of the stuff. You won't be able to get much stuff on the sled with Jose stretched out on it. And if we go without packs, we can travel faster."

I turned and looked at Tobie. She had a big grin on her face. "Of course I can get someone else to come with me, if you don't want to come back to this god-forsaken place!"

"Don't you dare!" I said. Then, very business-like, I added. "You wouldn't know where to find all my stuff. And we'll have to get Roger's stuff from Grizzly Valley, too, I suppose. And Jose's pack. It must be somewhere out there where I found him."

"It'll be Christmas vacation. We can take an extra day or two if we need it. Or, if you think it's too much work, or you're afraid we'll be lonely, I'm sure I could talk Roger into coming along to help!"

"You wouldn't!"

"Not if you treat me right. Now pull that sled over to the door of the tipi so we can slide Jose and the sleeping bag onto it."

There were still two medics camped at Woodbine trailhead when we got there. They checked Jose over, transferred him to a stretcher, and took off for Deaconess Hospital in Billings. We tied the sled on the top rack of Roger's car. Roger said he would wait for the four searchers who had gone out in the early morning. Tobie could take me back to Billings.

When we got to the hospital, there were reporters and photographers waiting. Tobie tried to make light of her part in the rescue. Said she was out searching and found my tipi. She was glad she had been there to help bring Jose in, but she emphasized the fact that I was the one who found him, and she gave me credit for bringing him out of the hypothermia. She obviously tried to keep her name out of it, but that night there was a lot of blab about it on TV, and the next morning both of our pictures were on the front page of the *Billings Gazette*.

Spring semester at Billings Senior High started off very differently from the one a year ago. Last year I had seemed to be invisible to the teachers and most of the students. This year even some of the teachers knew who I was. Students spoke to me in the halls and two of the fellows who had hazed me so much last year hunted for me in the lunchroom and asked a lot of questions about my three months in the wilderness. Frank said that this past fall he and Thomas had spent a weekend cross country skiing in Yellowstone, and asked if I would be interested in going along if they went again.

Of course I got snubbed by a few others, but I was glad to be back in school and was able to laugh it off.

My last class of the day was Ancient History with Mr. Johnson. I had been a little hesitant when they signed me up for it, but I was glad when I walked into class. Jose was there on crutches, and some of the girls gathered around us to talk. When Mr. Johnson told the class to sit down, Jose and I sat down but the four girls went up and sat in the front row. Nobody sat on the other side of me. I guess I was still a little touchy and wondered if I was being discriminated against. I was sitting there looking straight ahead, afraid to look around for fear of seeing the same expressions on the faces around me I had met in History class last year. Someone slipped into the seat beside me and I looked up. "Tobie!" I managed to keep the exclamation to a whisper—almost.

Tobie gave me a wink and a grin. "I thought you were ignoring me, Flint."

I laughed, and we both started to talk at once, till we heard Mr. Johnson's voice.

"I'm not seating you alphabetically this semester. You can sit where you please as long as you don't talk in class. If you do I'll move you." We didn't say another word.

Mr. Johnson told the class that he had decided the class would study ancient America. He looked at us again and said, "I think that Tobie and Flint and Jose can help us understand some of the early American cultures."

That made me think that he knew I had carried out the wilderness experience, and I hoped that he might say something about it after class, but he was too involved with other students. For the next couple of days, I kept trying to get up nerve enough to ask Mr. Johnson about the hundred dollars in bets that he was holding for me and to remind him that I had won the bet. Surely he knew that I had done what they had bet that I couldn't. I mentioned it to Tobie Friday after school when we took our run on the stairs at the University. I knew she wasn't as shy around teachers as I was, and I was hoping that maybe she would offer to mention it to him. But she just laughed and said, "Don't worry. He hasn't forgotten. He'll bring it up." I hoped so, because there were no Saturday auctions at the stock yards in January so I had no work, and I still had school supplies to buy.

Thursday of the following week, Mr. Johnson announced, "There won't be any homework tonight, or this weekend, because we're going to do something different in class tomorrow. I think you'll all enjoy it. It'll give us an introduction to other cultures."

I was going to ask Tobie what she thought it might be, till he added, "Tobie, would you please see me after class?" I scooted out real fast.

When I got home, Mom asked, "Flint, are you in some kind of trouble at school?"

"No, of course not, Mom. Why?"

"Are you sure?"

"I think so. What's up?"

"Well, the principal of your school called today. He wants me and your dad to come to his office at two o'clock tomorrow. He wouldn't tell me why, but he said it was important."

"I don't know what's wrong," I said, "but don't be worrying about it. It can't be very serious." I wasn't sure of that myself, but I told myself the same thing: there was no point in worrying. A year ago I'd have been scared to death, but time in the Beartooths must have given me more self-confidence, because I decided whatever was wrong, I could face it.

When I went to history class the next day, there was a sign on the door that said, "Ancient History class will be held in the gym today. Don't be late."

When I got to the gym, Roger and Frank were standing outside the door. They greeted me with a friendly "Hi, Flint," and asked, "Are you in this Ancient History class?"

"Yeah. What's up?"

"That's what we wanted to know. Our teacher said the principal had excused all the guys who were in American History last year from their last class this afternoon so they could go to the gym. What're you doing in class today that's so special?"

"I haven't the slightest idea."

When we stepped inside the gym several of the guys grouped around us and started asking about my time in the wilderness. We were interrupted by the booming of a bass drum. I turned and saw the drum lying on its side in the opposite corner of the gym. Sitting in chairs around it were six high school boys from Lame Deer school. I knew who they were, because I had been in school with them there two years ago, before we moved from the reservation to Billings. Standing in the corner behind them were Grandfather, my two aunts and three uncles, and several other adults from the Cheyenne reservation.

The drumbeats stopped and Mr. Woodenlegs, a member of the tribal council stepped out with a microphone in his hand. Jose hobbled along beside him on his crutches. "For those students who do not know the Cheyenne customs, it has always been a tradition that when a Cheyenne warrior comes home from a successful engagement, or has counted coup, or a young man has met a challenge that has earned him a place as a warrior of the tribe, we hold an honoring ceremony and a give-away in his honor. The principal of your school thought it appropriate that this time we hold it here, rather than on the reservation. He wants to expose some of the Billings students to this important part of the Native American culture. Will Flint Red Coyote please come forward?"

I'm sure my mouth dropped open, and I felt as though I wanted to run and hide, but I managed to walk across the floor in front of all those people. I wondered if they knew how much harder that was than pulling the sled across the snow with Jose on it. Maybe I should have stayed in the mountains!

Mr. Woodenlegs went on. "I am sure you all know that Flint continued to search for Jose Gonzales after others had given up hope, and was able to save Jose's life. Flint, can you tell the crowd a little about it?"

I felt tongue-tied. The boys on the drums saw how I felt, and probably thought about how they would feel. Anyway, they relieved the tension and gave me time to think by playing an honoring song on the drums, loud, soft, then loud again, ending in a loud boom.

"Thanks," I said, "but I didn't do it all. Tobie . . . " I saw Tobie in the crowd. She was looking at me, shaking her head "no." I remembered the valuable dolls she gave away secretly; how she had tried to minimize her part in the rescue. But I couldn't take all the credit for the rescue. "Tobie didn't give up either. She reached us in time to bring Jose out of the hypothermia, and helped bring him to the trailhead." I wanted to tell them what a life saver she really was, but I didn't dare.

Mr. Woodenlegs went on. "It is our custom to sing an honoring song and for our leaders to do an honoring dance around the pow-wow grounds, the gym this time, and all those who want to help honor the person fall in behind." As the drummers began beating the drums and singing the honoring song, Mr. Woodenlegs motioned for me to step in beside him as he began the Cheyenne slow-dance steps. As we circled the gym, with my parents and relatives following, I could see some of the students hesitating, telling others they didn't know the steps, but in the end they all walked onto the floor and fell in behind.

We circled the gym twice, then Mr. Woodenlegs took the mike again. "It is the custom of the Cheyenne people to give gifts, not to persons being honored, but in honor of them, to anyone who has helped them, either in this achievement, or in the past." Each of my aunts and uncles stepped forward with a blanket and several pieces of Indian beadwork, mostly necklaces and bolo ties. As Mr. Woodenlegs called out the names of each of the members of Search and Rescue who had still been at the trailhead when we arrived, my relatives handed them gifts. They presented other gifts to the principal of the senior high, my shop teacher, and the two Lame Deer teachers who had brought the students from the reservation.

Mr. Woodenlegs spoke again, "Although traditionally we give gifts in honor *of* the person, not *to* the person, in this case we do have something for Flint. Mr. Johnson?"

My history teacher stepped to the mike. "Last year, ten of my students each bet ten dollars to one dollar of Flint's, that Flint couldn't spend three fall and winter months alone in the wilderness, living off the land as his ancestors had done. I figured Flint would need that money for college, so I took a chance and invested the money in stock. It turned out well. So instead of the hundred dollars, I'm presenting him with a stock certificate worth a hundred and thirty."

The principal stepped forward. "Now I'd like to introduce Dr. Jon Reyhner from the Center for Excellence in Education at Northern Arizona University."

Northern Arizona U? That's where Tobie was going!

Dr. Reyhner stepped out and said, "Each year the Murwick Foundation provides the money for a four-year scholarship to be given to a deserving student who has done something outstanding for the public good. We had an application for admission that we hadn't paid much attention to until we got a call from one of your students whom we already knew. Then we received an e-mail from your principal telling us about Flint Red Coyote's challenge and the student he was recommending. Our scholarship committee held a quick meeting and we agreed upon who should receive it. I'm here to present that four-year scholarship to Flint Red Coyote."

I was so flabbergasted I couldn't say a word. I just reached out and took the paper he handed me and shook his hand.

The principal stepped to the mike and said, "Class time is nearly over. Students are dismissed to go home. Everyone started milling around and I noticed several of the students who had been so down on me last year heading over to get acquainted with the Cheyenne drummers!

"Wait! There's one more thing!" It was Mr. Woodenlegs on the mike again. "I knew Mr. Wolf Runner had a gift to give but he wanted to be the last one on the program."

Grandfather made his way out of the crowd and walked to the mike. "Will Tobie please come up here?" Tobie walked hesitantly forward and everybody watched as Grandfather lifted a large beaded necklace over her shock of curly hair and put it around her neck. Then he unfolded a large Native American pow-wow shawl and draped it over her shoulders.

Tobie took both his hands in hers, looked up at him with a smile, and said just one word, "Thanks." Then she turned to the crowd. "I don't have a blanket or beadwork to give away, but I do have something to give to Flint." She turned around, and right there in front of everyone she gave me a great big hug. I wanted to prolong it but, not in front of all those people! As I stepped back, she slid her hand down my arm and put something in my hand.

I looked down to see what it was. Three candy kisses!